The Gypsy Game

The Gypsy Game

ZILPHA KEATLEY SNYDER

A YEARLING BOOK

Published by
Bantam Doubleday Dell Books for Young Readers
a division of
Bantam Doubleday Dell Publishing Group, Inc.
1540 Broadway
New York, New York 10036

Visit us on the Web! www.bdd.com

Educators and librarians, visit the BDD Teacher's Resource Center at www.bdd.com/teachers

ISBN: 0-440-41258-7

Reprinted by arrangement with Delacorte Press

Printed in the United States of America

October 1998

10 9 8 7 6 5 4 3 2 1

OPM

*To everyone who asked for another game
with the same players*

One

"NOT VERY MUCH, I guess. Why?"

That was the first thing Melanie said when April asked her if she knew anything about Gypsies. April didn't answer. A minute or so later Melanie waved her hand in front of April's eyes and said, "Hey, anybody home? Come back to earth." Still no answer. April just went on staring into space.

They had been lying on their stomachs across the bed in April's room, digesting their Christmas dinners and talking about the presents they'd gotten and other Christmas stuff. Not talking all the time, but just once in a while when they felt like it. That was one of the good things about being the kind of friends they were. Sometimes, when they were together, they gabbed their heads off, and sometimes not. Either way it always felt okay.

So when it took a long time for April to say why she'd asked the Gypsy question, it didn't surprise Melanie all that much. She knew that when April's blue eyes got that spacey look it usually meant that she was on to something new and exciting, and if you waited long enough, you were sure to hear all about it. So Melanie waited. While she waited, she had time to sit up, scratch the mosquito bite on

1

her ankle, make a face at herself in the mirror on April's dressing table, and flop back down again.

Finally April sighed and said, "Oh, I don't know. It's just what you said about it not being the same. Going back and doing the same things over and over. You know, all that Egyptian stuff. And just the other day I was reading this magazine that had all this great stuff about Gypsies. I was just thinking how maybe we could . . ." She sat up, shoved back a straggle of blond hair, grinned at Melanie, and went on, "I was thinking that maybe we could try being Gypsies for a change."

If Melanie wasn't too thrilled by the idea right at first, it was probably just because she was so used to being Egyptian. Remembering, she kind of sighed.

April was watching her with narrowed eyes. "Well, what do you think?"

Melanie rolled over on her back. "Oh, I don't know. I was just remembering things, like that time Ken and Toby almost scared us to death."

"Yeah, the jerks," April said, but then she grinned too, and for a moment they both just lay there giggling like a couple of idiots. But then, at the very same moment, they both quit laughing and were quiet again, thinking and remembering. No one had said anything for quite a while when there was a knock on the door and then April's grandmother's voice, saying, "Girls. Marshall is here. May he come in?"

Melanie rolled her eyes. "Wouldn't you know it? Wouldn't you think that for once he'd be able to entertain himself for a few minutes, with all those new Christmas toys and everything?"

But April only shrugged. "Okay, Marshamosis, come on in," she yelled. A second later Melanie Ross's four-year-old brother appeared in the doorway, looking especially solemn and dignified in his Christmas bathrobe—red and black plaid with velvet tassels on the belt. The Rosses were African Americans, and both Melanie and Marshall had satiny brown skin and elegant black eyebrows, and today Marshall was looking even more handsome than usual. And—*no* pear-shaped velvet octopus dangling around his neck by two of its eight long legs.

Melanie poked April and whispered, "See. Like I told you. No Security!"

Marshall shut the door carefully behind him, walked across the room, climbed up on the bed, and asked in a businesslike tone of voice, "What are we talking about?"

April grinned. "Security," she said. "We were just saying, 'No Security.'"

Melanie poked April again and shook her head. Marshall didn't like being teased, and he particularly hated being teased about Security. As he started to climb down off the bed, his high-arched eyebrows were puckering together and his lips setting into a firm line. April grabbed him by the back of the shirt.

"Come on back, runt," she said. "I was just kidding. We weren't really talking about your precious Security. We were just talking about . . ." She stopped and grinned at Melanie. "Well, actually, we were talking about being Gypsies."

Marshall looked at April suspiciously.

"That's right," Melanie said. "We really were. April was just saying how maybe we could start playing a new

3

game—about being Gypsies this time instead of Egyptians."

"Gypsies?" Marshall's frown had returned. "Do Gypsies have pharaohs? I like being Marshamosis."

"But you'd like being a Gypsy, too," Melanie said. "You'd really like . . . well, you know, doing all those Gypsy things. Tell him, April. Tell him why he'd like being a Gypsy."

"Well, okay," April said. "Listen, Marshall. Gypsies are people who go around in caravans. A caravan is like—well, almost like a house trailer, only made of wood and pulled by horses. Or at least they used to be."

"Horses?" Marshall's forehead began to unpucker. Marshall, who had lived all his life in a city apartment where most pets weren't allowed, had this thing about all kinds of animals. Particularly big animals.

"That's right, horses." April thought a minute. "And some Gypsies train bears. That's how they make their living. They have trained bears who dance and do all kinds of tricks, and people pay money to watch the bears."

"Oh yeah?" Marshall's face was lighting up like neon when suddenly his eyes narrowed and the smile went out. "Bears?" he asked suspiciously. "Real bears, Melanie?"

Melanie nodded. If April said that Gypsies trained bears, they probably did. April had a special talent for that kind of information.

Marshall quit trying to scoot off the bed and sat back down between April and Melanie. He crossed his legs, smoothed out the front of his bathrobe, and straightened the velvet belt tassels. When he was all arranged, he said, "Okay. Let's be Gypsies. When do we get the bears?"

4

April rolled her eyes at Melanie and grinned. Melanie grinned back. "Okay," she said. "Bears." She got up and grabbed a pencil and a notebook off April's desk. It was the notebook they always took to their Egyptian business meetings to take notes about what they were going to do next and what kind of stuff they needed to bring the next time they went to Egypt. Turning to a new page, Melanie began to write. When she finished writing, she showed the page to Marshall.

"See," she said. "It says here, 'Bears!!! Get bears for Gypsy Game.'" She wiggled her eyebrows at April.

Marshall nodded approvingly. "Okay," he said. "Okay, let's be Gypsies. I get the first bear." He thought for a moment, his forehead wrinkling. "Where? Where do you get bears?"

The girls laughed. "Yeah," Melanie said. "Good question, Marshall." She looked at April and made her face say, "What do we do now?"

"Well." April nodded thoughtfully. "Well—yes! I guess the first thing we have to do now is—go to the library."

Marshall's eyes rounded in amazement. "They have bears at the library?"

That really cracked them up. By the time they'd stopped laughing, Marshall was mad again. He didn't like being laughed at. His lower lip was sticking out, and his forehead had started to pucker.

"No, Marshall," April finally gasped, "they don't have bears at the library. But we can find out about them there. About bears and Gypsies and all that stuff."

Marshall slid down off the bed. "Okay," he said. "Let's go. *Right now.*"

Of course they didn't go *right now* because libraries aren't open on Christmas Day, but before Melanie and Marshall went home that evening, it was all planned. On Thursday afternoon April would go down to the Rosses' apartment and get Melanie and Marshall. And then they would stop by to see if Elizabeth wanted to go, too. April wrote it down in her notebook: "GYPSIES 2:00 P.M. Thursday. Ask Elizabeth."

"But what about Ken and Toby?" Melanie asked. "Shouldn't we ask them if they want to be Gypsies? I mean, if we don't even ask, there's bound to be trouble."

April grinned happily. "Yeah, I know," she said. "Look out, Toby. Here comes trouble."

Actually, right at that moment, if anyone had asked Melanie what kind of trouble April was talking about, she probably would have said that April meant herself. That Toby was going to have "April trouble." But afterward, remembering exactly what April said that day, it occurred to Melanie that it was almost as if April had been doing the oracle thing again. As if she'd looked into the future and seen this big dark cloud of trouble heading in Toby's direction. Except that back then, on Christmas afternoon, not even a real oracle could have guessed how much, or how really weird, the trouble was going to be.

TWO

JUST AS THEY'D planned, April stopped by the Rosses' apartment on Thursday afternoon, and the three of them, April and Melanie and Marshall, went on down to pick up Elizabeth.

Elizabeth Chung was only a fourth grader, so when she first moved to the Casa Rosada, April and Melanie hadn't meant to invite her to join the Egypt Game. They finally did after Melanie's mom and April's grandmother had more or less insisted that they make the new girl feel at home. But then Elizabeth had turned out to be a great Egyptian. A little bit childish at times of course, but very enthusiastic about everything, and great at keeping her mouth shut around adults and other non-Egyptians. And when April had called up to ask if she'd like to be a Gypsy, she said yes right away.

"Oh yes," she said as soon as April explained what was going on. "I do. I will. Yes, I want to. When?"

"Well, we're planning to go to the library this afternoon to start doing the research," April said. "You know. We'll probably have to look up a bunch of stuff in encyclopedias and books. So bring some paper and a pencil. Okay?"

"Okay," Elizabeth said, her voice bubbling over with

7

enthusiasm and excitement. "Okay. Pencil and paper. Okay, I'll bring some. Okay."

April said good-bye and was about to hang up when Elizabeth said, "April, wait."

"Yeah," April said. "What?"

"What's a Gypsy?"

April had a hard time keeping from laughing out loud. "Look, Bethy," she said. "We'll tell you all about it on the way to the library. Okay?"

Later when April was telling Melanie about the telephone conversation, she imitated Elizabeth's high-pitched little-kid voice. " 'April. What's a Gypsy?' Can you believe it? She couldn't wait to start being a Gypsy before she even knew what one was."

But then Melanie pointed out that a lot of fourth graders probably don't know much about Gypsies. "Actually a lot of sixth graders don't either, I'll bet. And besides April . . ." Melanie smiled and tilted one eyebrow the way she always did when she thought somebody wasn't being very sensible. Or fair. Melanie had this thing about being fair. "And besides, April, you know Bethy just likes to do *whatever* we do."

April frowned. Even though Melanie was the best friend she'd ever had, she sure could be a drag when she wanted to. Like when she made you feel kind of mean for saying something mean about somebody, even though you didn't mean to be mean at all.

But by that afternoon when they started out for the library, April had forgotten all about being mad at Melanie. She was having too much fun telling everyone what it would be like being Gypsies. She didn't say too much about the horse-drawn caravans because she couldn't quite see how they could get hold of a horse—or a caravan either, for that matter. But there were a lot of Gypsy things they certainly could do. Like training animals and wearing Gypsy outfits, for instance.

"The men wear baggy pants and high boots and vests with all kinds of shiny things sewn on them, so they kind of glitter when they walk," she told them. "And the women wear these bright-colored head scarfs and all kinds of weird jewelry."

"Weird?" Marshall asked, frowning. "I don't like weird stuff. What about the bears?"

"Okay, Marshall. Bear info coming up. I'll get to bears in a . . ." Really focusing on Marshall for the first time, April noticed something. Security was back again, hanging around Marshall's neck by two of his legs, just like always. April nudged Melanie and pointed. "How come?" she whispered. "I thought you said he'd quit?"

Melanie only shrugged, so April reached over and tugged on one of Security's legs, which Marshall really hated for anyone to do. "Okay, Marshamosis," she said, "how come you brought the octopus? I thought you'd outgrown stuff like that."

Marshall jerked away and glared at April. "I did," he said. "I didn't want to bring him, but he wanted to come. Security likes libraries."

April might have had some more to say on the subject,

but Melanie poked her hard and shook her head. "The jewelry," she said. "Tell about the jewelry. What's weird about it?"

"Well, you know. They wear it kind of all over themselves. Like on their ankles and around their waists and foreheads. Oh yeah. And they tell fortunes." She looked at Melanie. "That's one of the best parts. They usually tell fortunes by palmistry. I can't wait to learn how to read people's palms."

"Yes," Melanie said. "Me too. I'd really like to tell fortunes. And what else, April? What other Gypsy things can we do?"

So April started telling them about training animals and juggling and dancing and things like that, but before she'd gotten anywhere near finished, they were already at the library.

To Mrs. George, who worked in the children's room, April and Melanie were still the Egyptian Girls, but as soon as she heard that they'd changed to Gypsies, she was enthusiastic about that, too. Before long the three girls were sitting at a table with lots of books and magazines and a couple of encyclopedias, and Marshall had gone off to the little kids' section with Mrs. George.

At first they started telling each other every time they learned something important. April told what she read about how the Gypsies had originally come from northern India, instead of from Egypt as most people thought. And Melanie found out that right now, in modern times, there were maybe a million Gypsies living in the United States. A little later they all got the giggles when they started trying to pronounce some words April found in an article about Romany, the Gypsy language. That got a little too noisy for a library, and after Mrs. George gave them a couple of serious glares, they started writing everything down. "Then we can meet in Egypt and read our notes about everything we found out," Melanie whispered.

"In Egypt?" Elizabeth asked. "I thought we were going to call it Gypsy now."

April laughed out loud and then covered her mouth with her hand when Mrs. George frowned in her direction. "Gypsy isn't a country," she said behind her hand. "Not like Egypt is a country. Gypsies don't have any particular country. That's the whole point about Gypsies. They just have, like, special places all over the world where they stay for a little while. Places called Gypsy camps."

"That's it, then," Melanie said. "We can change the name to the Camp. The Gypsy Camp. Everybody in favor say aye."

The vote was unanimous, three to nothing. "So it's official then," April said. "No more Egypt. From now on the Professor's backyard is officially the Gypsy Camp."

Right after the voting, which had gotten a little bit noisy, Mrs. George started frowning again, so they went back to writing—and making faces. April was reading about Gypsy fortune-telling, and she kept making faces that said things like "Hey, this is great" and "Wait'll you hear this." Elizabeth made faces too, but Melanie, who was reading a big fat book that Mrs. George had found in the adult department, just went on reading quietly with a strange look on her face. April was about to break the no-talking rule and ask what was the matter, when Marshall came back from the little kids' section carrying a bunch of books. Right away he began to be a nuisance.

"Where are the bears?" he kept asking, and "When can we get them?" and even "Who gets the daddy bear?"

At last Melanie gave up and said they'd better go. So they checked out a few of the best books, including a great one about reading palms and the big fat one from the adult department, and headed for home.

Three

THE FOUR OF THEM, April, Melanie, Elizabeth, and Marshall, were almost to the Casa Rosada when, just as they turned the corner onto Orchard Avenue, they ran into, of all people, Toby Alvillar. April was talking at the time and walking backward so that she could be sure Melanie and Elizabeth were listening. She had just said, "And they call themselves Roms, not Gypsies, and like I told you, they started out journeying hundreds of years ago from some place in India. At least that's what most people think. And they have their own laws and religion and language. . . ." She'd stopped then because she'd noticed that nobody was listening. Instead, they were staring past her at something or somebody over her left shoulder. She whirled around just in time to keep from bumping smack-dab into Toby.

Toby Alvillar's messy mop of hair hung down over his forehead, so that his oversized eyes peered out between curly brown strands. He was wearing a new Levi's jacket, probably a Christmas present, and one of his famous Alvillar grins. The kind that sometimes made April want to smack him one, right in the mouth.

"Well, well," Toby said. "What do you know? If it isn't February and Company." Toby had been the one who gave April the nickname February. Nobody else thought it was

13

very funny anymore, but Toby still seemed to. He looked around her at the other kids and asked, "What was old Feb telling you guys?" Nobody answered. In fact, nobody looked as though they were even thinking of answering. "Okay," Toby said. "Let's try an easier question. Where are you guys going?"

April's stare got even cooler. April Hall's cool stares were practically famous at Wilson School, but they never seemed to impress Toby all that much. "We're not *going* anywhere," she said. "We've already been."

"How about you?" Melanie asked. "Bet I can guess where you're going. Bet you're going to Ken's house."

"Well, you bet wrong," Toby said. "His whole family went skiing. Won't be back till Sunday."

"Oh yeah?" April said. "How come they didn't take you with them?" The Kamatas went skiing a lot in the wintertime, and once in a while, since Ken and Toby were best friends, they took Toby with them.

He shrugged. "They asked me, but my dad wouldn't let me go because we're too broke."

Marshall looked puzzled. He stared at Toby's legs and then at his arms. "Broke?" he asked. "Where? What broke?"

Toby laughed and patted his rear pocket. "Right here," he said, but Marshall went on looking worried. Toby tried again. "What I mean is moneywise, we are flat-out busted." He reached in his pocket and pulled out a five-dollar bill. "See this?" He waved the money in the air. "This is *it*. Our last red cent. My dad sent me to the store to buy something for dinner and then"—he threw up his hands dramatically—"that's all she wrote! The end! *Finito!* After that we starve to death."

Somebody, Elizabeth probably, gasped. April looked around. Sure enough, Elizabeth looked horrified, and even Melanie had a worried look on her face. April snorted. Couldn't they tell it was all just an act? Just some more typical Alvillar melodrama. She was willing to believe a bunch of weird stuff about old Alvillar. Like, for instance, the fact that his father was some kind of far-out hippie-type artist and sculptor and that he didn't have, and never had had, a mother and that he and his father lived in a terminally messy attic apartment with no furniture except for statues. But nobody had ever told April that Toby was starving, and she wasn't about to believe it now. However, it looked as if some people were willing to go along with almost anything old Alvillar said.

"Really?" Elizabeth's voice had a catch to it, like maybe she was about to cry. "You're really going to starve to death?"

Toby looked at Elizabeth. "Hey kid, don't worry about it," he said. "Maybe we won't starve clear to death. Who knows. Maybe my dad will finally sell a painting, or something. Or maybe he'll sell six paintings and a humongous statue, and next week we'll move to Palm Springs." He put the money back in his pocket and jumped up on the low cement wall beside the sidewalk. Holding out his arms like a tightrope walker, he started down the wall looking back over his shoulder. "Good-bye!" he yelled. "Good-bye forever."

They watched him go. Standing there in a clump on

the sidewalk, they watched as Toby went down the wall, balancing first on one foot and then the other. Suddenly he whirled around and came back toward them. When he was almost back to where he'd started, he stood on one foot, stuck the other way out behind, and bent forward like a gymnast on a balance bar. "Hey!" he said, teetering back and forth. "Are you guys going to . . ." He bent even farther, looked around cautiously as if he thought somebody might be listening, cupped his hands around his mouth, and whispered, "Egypt? Are you going to—*Egypt?*"

While April and Melanie were still staring at each other, trying to decide what to say, a loud, clear voice said, "Not Egypt. Egypt is all done." Melanie tried to shush him, but Marshall went right on. "We're going to be Gypsies now. With bears."

Toby fell off the wall. As soon as he picked himself up and dusted off his new jacket and the seat of his pants, he put his hands on his hips and stared at April and then at Melanie. "Okay. Tell all," he said. "What's this about Gypsies? What's up?"

At first April tried to pretend that Marshall didn't know what he was talking about. But Melanie didn't go along with it. Instead, she grabbed April's arm and pulled her a few yards down the sidewalk. Cupping her hands around April's ear, she hissed, "We might as well tell him. I don't want to lie about it. Not in front of Marshall."

"It would only be a temporary lie," April whispered back. "We'll tell him the truth pretty soon."

Melanie looked at Marshall and then shook her head

stubbornly. "Marshall's too young. He doesn't understand about temporary lies."

April gave up. "Okay, whatever," she said. "But Alvillar won't go along with it. I know he won't. Just you wait and see. This is going to be *war*." As they marched back to where Toby was waiting with Marshall and Elizabeth, she was imagining all the things that Toby would probably say. Like, "The Professor gave us the keys to *Egypt*, not to some old Gypsy hangout." Or else, "You guys can't just decide to change everything without telling me and Ken. We're Egyptians too, you know."

"Okay," she said to Melanie. "Talk. You think it's such a good idea, you tell him."

"Yeah, Ross," Toby said. "Talk."

Melanie nodded. "All right, I will. Look, Alvillar. We've been thinking of doing a thing about Gypsies. You know, just for a while, to see if everybody likes it. We were thinking that maybe we'd kind of run out of Egyptian things to do for the time being, anyway. So we've been reading about Gypsies. And we've been finding out all this neat stuff and . . ."

She glanced at Toby and immediately lost her train of thought. There was a very strange look on Toby's face. A kind of shocked and amazed expression, as if he'd just heard a tremendous explosion or else stuck his finger in an electric light socket. "Gypsies," he said finally in a breathless whisper. "You want to know about Gypsies? I don't believe it! I just don't believe it!" Backing up to the wall, he scooted up on it and sat there kind of laughing noiselessly and shaking his head back and forth.

Melanie and the little kids were all staring at him as if they were watching some kind of fascinating TV show. But April wasn't buying it. "Look, Alvillar," she said finally, "what are you raving about?"

"You want to know?" Toby turned his big high-powered eyes toward April. "You want to know what's so amazing?"

"Sure," April said scornfully. "Tell me. I can take it."

"Well," Toby said, "the truth is, you are right now, right this very moment, talking to one."

"One what?"

"One *Gypsy*," Toby said. "I am one. I, Toby Alvillar, am a real live, authentic, natural-born Gypsy. Have been all my life."

Four

WHEN TOBY ALVILLAR said he was a Gypsy, Melanie didn't know what to think. She knew what April was thinking because April said so, loud and clear. Which was that Toby was just shooting off his mouth and trying to get attention, like always. But Melanie wasn't so sure. Squinching up her eyes, she tried to picture him in a sparkly vest with a bright-colored sash around his skinny middle. The dreamed-up picture came easily: a Gypsy Toby, playing an accordion, while a bunch of trained bears . . .

The thought of *bears* brought her back to reality—and Marshall! Where was he? But actually he was still right there. Just sitting quietly on the wall listening to April and Toby argue.

"Yeah, sure, you're a Gypsy," April was saying. "And I'm Wonder Woman. Look, Alvillar, if you're an actual Gypsy, how come we've never heard about it before? Huh? Tell me that." She turned to Melanie and said, "Do you get it? I sure do. The very minute he finds out that we want to be Gypsies, he decides that he really is one. The only *real* one. So guess what that means. That means the only 'real' one gets to be, like, *king* of the Gypsies and decide what everybody else has to do."

It did sound pretty fishy, Melanie decided. "Can you prove it?" she asked. "Can you prove you're one?"

"Do you mean, like, do I have a card or something?" He reached into his pocket and pretended to pull out a card. "Yeah, sure. See, it says right here, 'Tobias Alvillar. Gypsy. First Class.'" He grinned and shrugged. "No, I guess I can't *prove* it, except that I'm a real authority on stuff about Gypsies. I can tell you all kinds of stuff about what they're like and how they live and why they travel around all the time. Hey, wait a minute. I *can* too prove it. My dad can tell you that we're Gypsies. Both of us. He's even more of a Gypsy than I am. Let's go ask him, right now. Okay?"

Melanie and April looked at each other. They looked at the little kids and then back at Toby. Finally they gave each other one of their almost invisible nods, which meant, "All right. Let's do it," and a second or two later all five of them were on their way to the Alvillars' apartment. But almost immediately Melanie, at least, was beginning to have some second thoughts about the whole thing. She was remembering some very strange rumors that she'd heard about Toby's lifestyle in general and about his father, Andre Alvillar, the artist, in particular. Rumors that, if they were true, might mean that the Alvillar apartment was not a good place to take a little kid like Marshall or a supersensitive one like Elizabeth.

Catching up with Toby, who was marching ahead like some kind of drum major, she said, "Hey, Toby. Maybe we ought to come some other time. Like, maybe you ought to give your dad some warning before you bring over a whole gang of kids. Besides, won't he be mad at you for not going to the grocery store?"

Toby shrugged. "He's probably forgotten about getting food by now. Artists are that way. Sometimes he forgets about food for days at a time." He turned to look at Melanie, and all of a sudden he began to grin. "And about warning him that we're coming . . . You don't have to worry in December. In the wintertime he wears overalls."

Melanie felt her face get hot. She looked away, wondering how Toby knew that one of the rumors she'd been thinking about was that sometimes his dad painted and sculpted without much on. Like almost naked, for instance.

Melanie wasn't too reassured by what Toby had said, but they were almost to University Avenue before she had a chance to talk privately to April. "Uh, April," she whispered. "I've been thinking—"

April pulled away impatiently. "Yeah? What?"

"Well, it's just that I've heard that Toby lives in a pretty weird place."

"Yeah, I know," April said delightedly. "Come on. I can't wait."

Melanie gave up. It would probably be all right. And besides, she really was curious to see if any of the rumors were true. She'd just have to be careful to keep an eye on Marshall. And Elizabeth, too.

Toby lived just off University Avenue on top of a building that was mostly a bar and pool hall. Only you didn't have to go through the downstairs to get up to where the Alvillars lived, which was good thing because no one was allowed in that part of the building who wasn't eighteen years old. Instead, you went around back and then up some outside stairs that ended on a rusty metal platform. At one end of the platform was a big metal door that wouldn't

21

open unless you kicked it. Toby kicked it once, and nothing happened.

"Back up," he said, "so I can get a run at it."

They all backed up, and Toby ran across the rattly slats of the platform, kicked, and the door crashed open. From somewhere in the distance a hollow-sounding voice said, "Great Caesar's ghost. What was that?"

"It's just me," Toby yelled, "and some friends! Can we come in?"

There was no answer, but he went in anyway. Melanie grabbed Marshall's hand and followed Toby into an enormous room, practically a block long and almost as wide. It had a very high ceiling that was partly made from glass, and on the floor, stretching from one side of the room to the other, was—*junk*. Most of the junk seemed to be from wrecking yards or construction sites, but mixed in with the pipes and rods and wheels were bicycle handlebars, lampshades, stovepipes, birdcages, telephones, frying pans, and a bunch of pink plastic toilet seats. Some of it was woven and twisted and welded together into strangely threatening shapes with staring eyes and clawlike hands. Some of it was piled into tall, teetering towers like the metal skeletons of ancient castles. But most of it was just scattered around or stacked up in great, dusty piles.

Melanie pushed Marshall back behind her and held him there as they moved forward, following Toby between two junk piles and, at one point, under the huge blue body of what looked like an almost life-sized brontosaurus.

Marshall liked the brontosaurus. Hanging back, he pointed up at the tiny head at the end of a long arching neck that seemed to be made of hundreds of welded-together Chicken Of The Sea tuna cans. "Dinosaur," he whispered. "Stop. I want to see the tuna dinosaur." But Melanie kept pulling him after her as she followed Toby between the barrel-shaped legs and under the huge blue body.

From there they wound their way through several other junk-pile jungles. Here and there among the piles Melanie noticed what might possibly be considered a living area: in one place a kind of platform with a mattress and a bunch of blankets scattered around over it; and in another, a table covered with dirty dishes not far from a greasy-looking gas stove with a gaping, doorless oven. Just beyond the kitchen area they finally came to a stop beside a tall, extremely hairy man dressed in a baggy sweatshirt and incredibly dirty overalls. The man had a paintbrush in one hand and a pallette covered with blobs of paint in the other, and behind him on the wall was a very strange painting of animals that seemed to be half human. Or perhaps humans that were half animal.

"Hi, Dad," Toby said. "These are the guys I told you about. The ones who have the other keys to the Professor's backyard. You know, besides Ken and me."

"Aha," the hairy man said. "I see. I—see." But he didn't see, at least not right away, because for the longest time he went on staring at the painting before he looked or even moved. And when he finally did turn around, he very slowly put down his palette and brush, pulled up a chair, and sat down and stared.

It was a weird feeling, coming into someone's home, if

you could call an enormous attic junkyard a home, and having them just sit down and stare at you. Melanie glanced around to see how the others were taking it. Elizabeth looked as though she was about to make a run for it. Melanie put her free arm, the one that wasn't wrapped around Marshall, across Elizabeth's shoulders. And April? April was wearing the deadpan she used around most adults, so for once Melanie couldn't tell what she was thinking.

"These dudes came to ask you something," Toby was saying. "I told them that we were Gypsies, but they won't believe me. So could you just tell . . ."

Just then his father got up, came over to where they were all standing, took Marshall by the shoulders, and pulled him away from the others. Melanie grabbed for Marshall's hand, missed, started to say something, and stuttered to a stop. Mr. Alvillar was leading Marshall over to stand near the huge picture that was painted on the wall. Putting his hand under Marshall's chin, he turned his face toward the light and pulled Security around so that his fuzzy pear-shaped head was hanging down in front. "There," he said. "Perfect. Don't move a muscle." To Melanie's amazement Marshall did as he was told. Standing very still, Marshall lifted his chin so that the light from the glass ceiling spilled down across his face, turning his skin to dark-brown velvet and making small circular shadows under his long black eyelashes.

Mr. Alvillar picked up a pencil and a small notebook and began to draw, glancing up at Marshall now and then. "Beautiful," he said once or twice. "Perfectly beautiful."

April stepped forward determinedly. "Mr. Alvillar—"

she started, but before she could say any more, Toby moved between her and his father. Shaking his head, Toby put his finger to his lips.

"Just a minute," Toby whispered. "It won't take him long."

He was right. After two or three minutes Mr. Alvillar put the notebook down, went over to where Marshall was standing, and put out his hand. Marshall shook hands solemnly and then turned to look behind him at the mural of animal-humans and human-animals. He studied it carefully before he asked, "Am I going to be in that picture?"

"Would you like to be?" Mr. Alvillar asked.

Marshall nodded thoughtfully. "Can I be an octopus? Or else a bear. Can I be a bear?"

Mr. Alvillar didn't laugh or even smile. Glancing from Marshall to the wall, he nodded slowly. "Yes. A bear. A strong bear, I should think." Then he picked up his brush and palette and went back to staring at the wall.

"Dad," Toby said, and then more loudly, "Dad! Could you tell these guys something? Could you tell them about how we're both natural-born Gypsies? Okay? I already told them, but they didn't believe me."

Toby's dad waved briefly as if he were brushing away a fly and went on staring at the painted wall.

The whole thing—the mysterious attic apartment, the strange statues, and Toby's weird, paint-smeared father— was making Melanie feel more and more uneasy. Grabbing Marshall by the back of his shirt, she pulled him away, and, catching April's eye, she tried to make her face say, "Let's get out of here." But just about then Toby's dad snapped out of his trance and began to talk, and April didn't want to leave.

"Shhh," she whispered. "Listen."

So they stayed a minute longer to hear what Toby's father would say.

Five

APRIL WAS REALLY amazed to hear that Toby hadn't been lying after all. At least not completely. What his father actually said, after Toby finally got through to him, was, "Yes, I suppose you could put it that way." He nodded solemnly, looking at April and Melanie. "My mother, Toby's grandmother, was born in Romania, of Gypsy parents. So that would make Toby one-quarter Gypsy." He smiled at April. "Is that what he said?"

"Well, yes. Pretty much," April said. "He said he was a natural-born Gypsy and that he knew all kinds of stuff about Gypsies. Like he was a real authority, or something."

"Oh, did he?" Mr. Alvillar looked at Toby with a familiar kind of obnoxious gleam in his strange dark eyes. It was easy to see where Toby got his looks, not to mention his aggravating disposition.

"An authority?" Mr. Alvillar said. He combed his curly black beard with one paint-smeared hand, leaving a slightly purple streak next to a whitish one that might have been natural. "Well, I don't know if I'd go so far as to say that. Never has shown too much interest in the subject before now."

"Yes, I have," Toby said indignantly. "Remember that

time you got invited to that Gypsy get-together in Oakland? And I wanted to go too?"

Mr. Alvillar picked up his paintbrush and palette and stared at his mural for a moment before he answered. "Ah yes, so you did. Right after I told you about the banquet. You seemed to be quite interested in the banquet, as I recall."

Toby and his father were still arguing about why Toby had wanted to go to the Gypsy convention when Melanie grabbed Marshall's hand, motioned to April and Elizabeth, and headed back through the junk piles in the general direction of the outer door. April followed reluctantly. Just before they got out of earshot, they heard Toby saying, "Okay, so I did want to go to the banquet. I thought if we did, maybe you'd learn something about Gypsy cooking."

"Gypsy cooking? How do you know you'd like Gypsy cooking?"

"I don't know." Toby's voice was fading away in the distance. "But I figured anything would be better than all that canned tuna."

After they could no longer hear the arguing voices, they lost their bearings and found themselves wandering around between some unfamiliar-looking junk piles. It was beginning to feel a lot like trying to get out of a maze. No matter which way they turned, they seemed to keep coming back to the particularly confusing jungle of junk that surrounded the enormous blue brontosaurus. Again and again they found themselves staring up at its incredibly long neck with its tuna-can vertebrae, then ducking under its immense blue body and squeezing between its huge barrel-shaped legs. They must have passed the dinosaur at least three times before they took a sudden left turn and found themselves right by the big metal door. It wasn't quite so hard to open from the inside.

So it turned out that Toby really was a Gypsy. At least a little bit. Only about one-quarter actually, which wasn't really enough to give him any special rights. That was what April said anyway. That was what she told Melanie on the way home, and it was also what she said to Toby when he called up the next day.

April had been surprised and a little bit embarrassed when her grandmother said there was a young man on the phone who wanted to speak to April Hall.

"Who is it?" April asked.

"I'm not sure," Caroline said. "He didn't give his name, but I would guess it's one of your Egyptian friends. Sounded like the one with all that curly hair."

"Not Toby?" April asked, but it was, of course, and what he wanted to know was when the next Gypsy meeting was going to be.

"Well, maybe tomorrow afternoon," she said, "but maybe not. Why?"

"Why? Because I'm coming. And wait till you see what I'm going to bring. I've got lots of old books and photographs. Oh yeah, and some antique Gypsy jewelry that used to be my grandmother's."

Until Toby mentioned the jewelry, April had been frantically trying to think of some way to keep him from coming, at least until Ken was back from skiing. It would be a terrible nuisance to have him there when they were just trying to set up the beginning rules and ceremonies for the new game. But, on the other hand, the antique Gypsy jewelry did sound pretty interesting. She wished there was some way they could have the jewelry without having Toby, but obviously there wasn't. Finally she broke down and admitted that they were definitely planning to meet the next day at three o'clock, as soon as Marshall got back from day care.

But then she went on to tell him that she and Melanie had decided that being one-quarter Gypsy wasn't enough to get him any special privileges, so he'd better not count on it. And Toby just laughed and said he didn't need any special privileges. After he hung up, April called Melanie.

"Nothing good," she answered when Melanie asked, "What's up?" "It looks like old Alvillar's going to be there tomorrow for sure. I thought maybe he'd at least wait until Ken gets back, but no such luck."

Melanie didn't say anything for a minute, and when she did, she sounded different, kind of flat and unenthusiastic. Almost as if she'd changed her mind about the whole Gypsy Game idea. "Well, maybe we ought to think about being Gypsies some more before we decide for sure," she said.

April couldn't believe it. "Hey, what's with you, all of a sudden?" she asked. "I thought you really liked the idea a lot."

"Well, yes, I did before . . ." She stopped then, and she wouldn't say "before" what. But she seemed to get a little bit interested again after April told her about all the things Toby was going to bring. "Real Gypsy stuff?" she said. "That's cool."

"Yeah. If he really meant it," April said. "With Alvillar

you never know if he's going to do what he says he's going to do."

But this time he did, and then some. He was there all right, not just on time, but early, which was very unusual for Toby Alvillar. When April, Elizabeth, Melanie, and Marshall (with Security again) arrived at the storage yard, they knew at once that he was already there. The Professor's shiny new padlock was just hanging there wide open, and the gate was slightly ajar. And when they went in, there was Toby sitting on the floor of the storage shed. Behind him was what looked like a real Gypsy caravan, an elaborately carved and painted wooden house on wheels. April heard a gasp of surprise and then realized it had come from her own throat.

"Yeah," Toby said when he saw their faces, "pretty amazing, isn't it. My dad did it last night."

As they got closer, they realized that it wasn't a real Gypsy caravan but only a picture of one painted on a huge piece of cardboard tacked to a wooden frame so it could stand up by itself. A beautifully painted almost life-sized copy of a Gypsy caravan, with steps leading up to an open door and up above a steeply pitched roof with a stovepipe sticking out on one side. As they all stood there staring, Marshall climbed up into the shed, peeked around the cardboard, and then disappeared behind it. When he came out the other side, he said, "Huh! It's just an old picture."

Toby laughed. "Right on, Marshall," he said. "It's a picture all right. But a new one, actually. My dad just painted it last night." He sighed. "The whole humongous thing. He was about to start making dinner, see, and I was fooling

31

around with a chest of stuff that belonged to my grand-mother, and I found this little picture postcard of a Gypsy caravan. I just showed him the picture, and that did it. All of a sudden he was dragging out this huge hunk of card-board and starting to paint."

"It's beautiful," Elizabeth said. "For a minute I thought it was real."

"Me too," Melanie said.

Toby put his hands on his hips and stared at the picture. "Yeah. I guess so. I sure wasn't too crazy about it last night. Had to make my own dinner." He sighed. "Artists are like that. Mostly you can't get their attention, and when you do, you wish you hadn't."

April laughed, and when Toby looked at her curiously, she asked, "Like with your Halloween costume?"

Toby laughed. "Yeah. Exactly. At first he couldn't be bothered, but then he got this idea of turning me into some kind of new art form, and the first thing I knew, I was completely packaged and labeled."

That made everyone laugh, so, as it turned out, the first Gypsy meeting started out with everybody in a pretty good mood. But that was just the first few minutes. After that things went downhill pretty fast.

Six

THE FIRST QUARREL was about fortune-telling. April just happened to mention that only girls would get to be fortune-tellers because that's the way it was with real Gypsies. The women told fortunes, and the men were blacksmiths or mechanics or musicians or animal trainers or other things like that. And then Toby said that he could be a fortune-teller if he wanted to.

"I'd be great at telling fortunes," he said. "Besides, if you can pretend you're a Gypsy, I can pretend I'm a fortune-teller." Arching an eyebrow, he added, "At least *I* don't have to pretend I'm a Gypsy."

April threw up her hands. "See, there he goes," she said to Melanie. "I told you he was going to pull this 'Who's the *real* Gypsy' stuff on us."

Elizabeth cooled that fight by suggesting that there could be a fortune-telling contest, and the winner, the one who told the best fortunes, would get to be the first official fortune-teller.

For a fourth grader Elizabeth was really amazingly good at thinking up peaceful ways to settle things. Melanie thought it was pretty smart of Elizabeth to realize that April and Toby would love the idea of having a fortune-telling contest because they were both so sure they could think up the world's most exciting fortunes. So the fortune-teller quarrel ended peacefully, but the next big problem wasn't so easy to solve.

The next argument was about whether or not Gypsies stole things. It started when it was April's turn to tell what she'd found out at the library. One of the things she said was, "The Gypsies in Europe never got to stay in any camp very long because they got chased out by the people who already lived in that part of the country."

"Why?" Marshall asked. "Why did they chase them?"

"Well, because they looked different and had different customs. And because they stole things—"

"Or because people *said* they stole things," Toby interrupted.

April put her hands on her hips and glared at Toby. "It's my turn to talk. I thought we said we were going to take turns."

"Yeah. To talk," Toby said. "Not to tell lies."

"It is *not* a lie. I read a book that said that Gypsies had very strict rules about not stealing from each other but that they thought it was all right to steal from the Gadje. Gadje," she repeated, looking at Marshall and Elizabeth. "That's what they call all the people who aren't Gypsies, remember?"

"Well, that's not what my dad says," Toby said. "And besides, what else were they going to do? There were laws that said they weren't allowed to own land or have any real jobs. So sometimes they either had to steal or starve. But lots of the time they just got blamed for things other people stole. Sometimes other people stole things and blamed it on the Gypsies because they knew everybody would believe that Gypsies were guilty. My dad says that happened a lot back in the olden days when my grandmother was living in Romania."

"I know." Melanie was nodding. "I read about it. Lots of things like that happened. And worse things, too. Things like—"

But Toby interrupted. He was waving his hands around as he talked, and his voice was getting higher and tighter. "Yeah, you know. I mean, people are like that. That's what my dad says. People just like to blame everything on someone else so they won't have to admit that anything's their own fault." Then he looked right at April and said, "Like how some female types always blame everything that goes wrong on some poor innocent guy and—"

That was about as far as he got before April grabbed him by the front of his shirt. But Melanie pulled her away. "Hey, cool it," she said to April. She thought for a moment before she added, "Besides—he's right about blaming other people. My mom says the same thing. She says all kinds of people waste too much energy blaming everything on other kinds of people."

Toby inspected the front of his shirt. "Yeah," he said. "I totally agree. So I won't blame you for tearing my shirt." He gave April one his most maddening grins. "Not until I talk to my lawyer, anyway."

April's fists were clenched and she was still breathing hard when she heard Elizabeth saying, "Toby! Toby! Did you bring all the Gypsy stuff you were going to show us? We can't wait to see it. Can we, April?"

"Huh?" Toby stared at Elizabeth blankly for a second before he said, "Oh yeah. The Gypsy stuff. Yeah." All of a sudden he was grinning as if nothing had happened. He seemed to have forgotten all about being mad, or about teasing either. "Hey, just wait till you see this stuff."

As she watched Toby taking off his backpack, April was thinking, *What a wishy-washy wimp he is—right in the middle of a good fight one minute, and then* . . . But as Toby began pulling fascinating things out of his backpack, she lost her train of thought.

First there was a beautiful embroidered shawl with a long silky fringe, and as Toby unwrapped it, a lot of silvery jewelry set with colored stones spilled out. There were bracelets, necklaces, anklets, headbands, and belts, most of which were set with colored jewels and had dangling streams of glittering spangles.

"Wow!" Melanie said. "This stuff is gorgeous." She was hanging a silver filigree band set with green stones around her forehead so that the large center stone hung down almost to her eyebrows. "Look, April," she said. "How do I look?"

April looked up from where she was trying to fasten a band of spangles around her ankle. "Great. Wow. That looks great." Forgetting about the anklet, she stood up and adjusted the band on Melanie's forehead. Then she stood back to admire the effect. To admire the way the green stone, gleaming in the center of Melanie's smooth brown forehead between her arching black eyebrows, turned her into something beautifully strange and foreign-looking. Before long they were all adorned with bracelets, anklets, and headbands. Even Marshall was wearing a long shiny necklace.

Elizabeth, running her fingers over her necklace, started to say, "It makes me feel just like . . ."

April and Melanie finished the sentence in unison: ". . . a Gypsy."

Of course that was it. Somehow putting on the beautiful old Gypsy jewelry made the difference, and for the first time they were all feeling almost as much like Gypsies as they had felt like Egyptians.

But then Toby said they had to take it all off. "My dad said I could borrow it to show you but that I'd have to bring it right back," he said.

They hated to give it up. April was handing her necklace back to Toby when suddenly her eyes narrowed. "So, how come you told us you guys were going to starve to death when all the time you had all this expensive jewelry?"

Toby snorted. "That," he said, "is one stupid question, February. In the first place you can't eat jewelry. And in the second place my dad would never sell it. Not in a million years. And in the third place all those stones are just colored glass. I mean, you don't think Gypsies are rich enough to own real rubies and emeralds, do you?"

April was glaring. "Well, maybe not. Not unless they stole them, anyway."

By the time Melanie and Elizabeth broke up that fight, it was four-thirty and past time for Elizabeth and the Rosses to be back home. So everybody got ready to leave by gathering up all their own personal Egyptian stuff that didn't seem likely to fit into a game about Gypsies.

Melanie took the Crocodile Stone because she'd been the one to find it, as well as her blown-glass figurines that had been on the altar of Isis. And April got the papyrus scrolls out from their hiding place under the statue of Diana. Everyone had worked on the scrolls at one time or another, but since she'd been the one to contribute the onionskin paper, she figured they belonged to her.

At first Toby said he didn't want anything except Thoth, his stuffed owl, but later he wrapped up the cat skull and the dead tarantula and took them, too.

After that they all went home without coming to any decision about what to do next, except that they would meet again the next afternoon. Which was just fine except that the Kamata family would be back from skiing by then, and that meant a whole new set of problems to deal with. Problems like how to turn Ken, who was so good at being himself, into a Gypsy just as he was finally beginning to feel comfortable being Egyptian.

That was what April told Melanie and Marshall as they were saying good-bye outside the Rosses' apartment. "It's not going to be easy," she said. "I mean, getting Kamata to change."

"Yeah," Melanie said. "Don't I know it." Then she grinned and hit herself on the forehead and said, "*Sheesh!*" the way Ken always did.

April did the same thing and then ran on upstairs.

Seven

THAT NIGHT APRIL called Melanie and asked her to come up after dinner to work on plans for the Gypsy Game, but Melanie said she couldn't. Her father had an evening class, and her mother was going to a teachers' meeting, so she had to stay home with Marshall. "Why don't you come down here?" she said. "You can help me baby-sit."

So April took all the library books and went down to the Rosses'. Marshall had already been put to bed, so they could have gotten started right away, except that Melanie kept thinking of other things to do. Things like making hot chocolate and reading the comics and even watching part of a stupid TV show that she usually said she hated. April was puzzled. But when she asked Melanie what was the matter, she only shrugged.

"I don't know," she said. "Maybe I'm just not in the mood." And she went on being not in the mood until April got out the book on palm reading. The book was called *The Art of Palmistry*, and it turned out to be pretty interesting. It told all about the history of palm reading and also had lots of diagrams that showed which lines were supposed to tell about which important parts of a person's life.

At first they checked out each other's life lines, both of

which seemed to be nice and long, which was supposed to be very important. And their head lines were deep and fairly straight, which meant that they didn't have any serious mental problems. According to the book a lot of wiggles and breaks in your head line might mean that you were a little bit weird.

"I guess we're both boringly normal," Melanie said.

"Yeah, too bad." April shrugged. "Hey, I know. Do you suppose Marshall's still awake? I wonder what his palm looks like. I mean, you'd have to say he's a little bit weird. Like still having a security object when he practically acts like an adult in most other ways."

"Well, okay, if he's not asleep already." Melanie seemed a little uncertain. "But don't you say anything about Security to him, April. My dad says teasing just makes it worse. You know he'd just about stopped needing Security until people started teasing him about it." Melanie smiled when she said "people," but April got the point. After she'd promised she wouldn't do any teasing, they tiptoed into his room to see if he was still awake.

Actually Marshall was still very much awake. In fact, he wasn't even in the room. Security was there, however, all tucked in with his head on the pillow. But Melanie didn't seem worried. "The kitchen," she said. "He'll be in the kitchen."

Sure enough, there Marshall was, standing on a chair by the kitchen counter, smearing honey and peanut butter all over two pieces of bread, not to mention his hands and the front of his pajamas. He didn't seem to mind when Melanie said they wanted to practice their palm reading on him. In fact, he seemed quite pleased. The only problem was he refused to wash his hands.

"Why not, for heaven's sake?" Melanie asked. "Just look at them. Ugh!"

"Because I haven't finished yet." He licked a honey-coated finger thoughtfully. "My feet aren't gooey," he said. "You could read my feet."

So Marshall sat down on the chair and stuck out his feet, and while April and Melanie studied his soles, he went on eating his sandwich. The only trouble was that the book didn't say anything about foot-reading techniques, and all the lines seemed to be in different places. So finally they just made up some stuff about how he was going to grow up to be king of the Gypsies and president of the United States and maybe even an animal trainer in the circus. After that he let them clean him up and put him back to bed.

When they finally got back to the palmistry book, they found some neat things about how to tell how many times you'd be married and how many kids you'd have. But when they tried reading those lines on each other's palms, they didn't get very far because neither one of them seemed to have any lines in the right places. They'd just about decided that eleven was a little too young for marriage lines, when Melanie's mother came back from her teachers' meeting. She looked pretty exhausted, so April said good-bye and went on home. As she went out the door, she whispered, "Don't forget. Tomorrow. *The Return of the Great Kamata!*"

Sure enough, when Toby arrived at the storage yard the next day, Ken was with him—and they were late, as usual.

Elizabeth was away visiting relatives, but April and Melanie had been waiting, sitting at the edge of the shed floor, for at least half an hour. Marshall, with Security hanging around his neck, was digging in the dirt with a pointed stick. April had just said something about people who were always late, when suddenly there they were, Ken and Toby, looking like *Ta-da!* *Toby Alvillar and Ken Kamata have arrived, you lucky people!* Closing the gate behind them, they sauntered over to the shed.

Toby was grinning. "I already told him all about what's happening," he said. "And it's okay. He's cool about doing the Gypsy thing. Aren't you, Kamata?"

Ken only shrugged and went on swaggering around with his hands in the pockets of his new expensive-looking sports jacket. Ken had always been like that. The kind of supercool guy who knew he didn't have to say anything to get everybody's attention. Everybody watched while he looked at the new Gypsy caravan mural and then at the stripped-down Egyptian altars of Thoth and Isis and Set. When he got to Set's altar, he picked up his fake dagger and his shrunken head, looked at them carefully, and stuffed them in his pockets.

April was getting mad. Who did he think he was, swaggering around without saying a word, while everybody stared at him. "Well, what do you think, Kamata?" she asked, biting off each word angrily.

Ken slowly turned his head, looking all surprised, as if he couldn't imagine what she was talking about. "Think? What do I think about—what?"

April took a deep breath and unclenched her teeth enough to say, "About—being—Gypsies!"

Ken leaned against one of the temple pillars, pulled out the shrunken head, and began to toss it up and catch it. "I'm thinking," he said. "I'll let you know when I decide."

"They wear really neat clothes," Melanie said. "You know, fancy embroidered things with lots of jewelry and . . ."

"Jewelry! Holy cow!" Ken said.

"And they play musical instruments," Melanie added. Everybody knew that Ken played the trombone in the school band and that music was one more thing he was just naturally great at.

"Oh yeah?" Ken looked mildly interested. "They play trombones?"

After Melanie admitted that she wasn't sure if Gypsies played trombones, Ken went back to playing with the shrunken head. Tossing it up, catching it, and . . .

"Hey," April said suddenly, "and juggling. Sometimes they do juggling."

"Oh yeah?" Ken said again. "And what else?" He looked at Marshall, who had come over to watch how the shrunken head's long black hair streamed behind it when Ken tossed it into the air. "What else do Gypsies do, Marshamosis?"

"They can read your feet," Marshall said.

April and Melanie laughed. "He's talking about fortune-telling," Melanie said. "You know, palmistry."

"Yeah, palmistry," April added. "That means telling your fortune by reading your palm. Here, I'll show you. Give me your hand and . . ."

Ken stuffed his hands and the shrunken head back into

his pockets. "No you don't," he said. "Nobody's going to read my palm."

"No, I mean it," April insisted. "We can read your palm. Can't we, Melanie?" She grabbed Ken's arm and tried to pull his hand out of his pocket. But he only jerked away, shoving April with his elbow. Shoving her so hard she stumbled backward, tripped over the sacred fire pit, and sat down—hard.

When April got to her feet, her fists were clenched and her eyes were fiery. She had swung once, missed, and was getting ready to try again when Melanie grabbed her arms and pulled her away. Toby grabbed hold of Ken. For a few seconds nobody spoke or moved. A few very long seconds—until suddenly the strained silence was interrupted by an unfamiliar sound that seemed to be coming from just outside the gate. A bumping and snuffling and scratching that started and stopped and then started up again. It was an entirely unfamiliar noise. Unfamiliar, unexpected, and weirdly nonhuman.

The girls were still clutching each other, but for a different reason now, and Ken and Toby seemed to be doing almost the same thing. But nobody was holding on to Marshall. So while the big kids clutched and stared, Marshall ran to open the gate.

"Don't, Marshall. Wait a minute." Melanie's voice was sharp and urgent. But she was too late. Marshall had already unlatched the gate and opened it enough to peek out.

For an endless minute he stared out through the narrow opening without moving or saying a word while Melanie said, "Come back here, Marshall," and everyone else said things like, "What is it?" and "What's out there?"

44

After what seemed like a very long time, Marshall finally began to move. Pushing the gate slowly shut, he tiptoed back toward the shed. They could see his face then, and it was easy to tell that he was absolutely out of his mind with—happiness? When he was almost to the shed, he pointed back toward the gate and whispered, "It's my bear. My bear came."

Eight

"A *BEAR?*" someone yelled, and a second later they were all at the gate, trying to peek out without opening it wide enough to let a bear, or whatever, come through. Toby had gotten there first, but Ken, who was bigger, had the best view. All the rest of them were squeezed in underneath. For a minute there was no sound except some grunting and griping as people got pushed and stepped on. It was Ken who spoke first.

"It's nothing but a dog," he said. "*Sheesh*, Marshall. It's just a big dog." Stepping backward, he yanked the gate open, tumbling people in every direction. Sitting on the ground with Melanie beside her and Toby sprawled across both of their legs, April looked up in time to see a weird-looking creature standing in the wide-open gate. For several seconds it just stood there turning its big black head from side to side, staring at them. At least, it *seemed* to be looking at them. There was no way to tell for sure. Its eyes, if it had any, were completely covered by a thick, furry mop of black hair.

Marshall got back on his feet and shoved past Ken. A few feet away from the shaggy creature, he stopped and stared, and the creature stared back. Or at least turned its eyeless face in Marshall's direction. "It's not either a dog," he said confidently. "It's my bear."

Moving forward, he held out his hand, and before Melanie could shove Toby off her legs and stagger to her feet, he reached out to pat the shaggy bump that seemed to be its head. And as he patted one end of the big black hairball, at the other end what had to be a tail, a short stubby tail, began to wag.

Well, of course it was a dog. Everyone knew that immediately. Everyone, that is, except Marshall.

"Hello, Bear," Marshall was saying. As he went on patting, a long red tongue emerged from the hairy mop and licked his face. Marshall giggled happily.

Melanie looked at April, making an especially desperate "what do we do now?" face. April knew what she meant. She was asking April to help her think of a way to keep Marshall from being absolutely wiped out when he learned that his bear was only an extremely shaggy black dog. "Well, anyway, Marshall, it sure looks like—" April was starting to say, when Toby interrupted.

"Yeah," he said, "Marshall's right. That's a bear all right." He stepped forward, stuck out his hand, and let it be licked by the red tongue. "See that? That is definitely a bear's tongue. A Gypsy bear," he told Marshall. Turning back toward the others, he added, "That's the way Gypsy bears always look. They breed them to look that way on purpose, so if the cops start getting after them for keeping a wild animal, they can just say, 'What do you mean, wild animal? This here is only a very special Gypsy breed of dog.' "

Ken laughed. "Sure it is," he said. "Well, all I can say is, if that four-legged dust mop is a—" But before Ken could finish the sentence, Toby had grabbed him and was whispering in his ear. As Toby whispered, Ken shook his head, then nodded, grinned, and said, "Yeah, I gotcha. Okay, Alvillar, I think you're right. That is definitely a Gypsy bear. Best-looking Gypsy bear I ever saw."

Toby looked at April. "So," he said. "Now that we have us a bear—"

"It's *my* bear," Marshall interrupted.

"Right," Toby said without missing a beat. "Like I was saying, now that this kid's got himself a bear, what kind of Gypsy bear tricks are we going to teach him to do?"

April eyed him suspiciously. "You're the one with a Gypsy grandmother. What kind of tricks did your grandmother teach you?"

For the next ten minutes or so, April and Toby argued about what kind of tricks Gypsy bears usually did and whether they could teach them to Marshall's bear. And while they were arguing, Marshall coaxed the big shaggy—whatever—into the yard and shut the gate behind him.

"Come on, Bear," Marshall kept saying, and the "bear's" ears would go up and he would go where Marshall wanted him to.

The dog-bear did seem to like Marshall best, but the weird thing was that he seemed to react whenever anyone called him Bear. Whenever anyone said, "Here, Bear," he would bounce over to that kid and try to lick him or her in the face. Before long everyone was getting into the act, particularly Toby, who started trying to teach Bear to dance on his hind legs, something that, according to Toby, all Gypsy bears were supposed to do.

"Here, watch this," he said. Holding up Bear's front paws, he made him walk around on his hind legs. Bear didn't seem to mind. With his tongue lolling out of one corner of his mouth and his head cocked to one side, he shuffled happily around on his hind feet. "Look, he's dancing!" Toby yelled. He waltzed Bear around two or three times before he turned him loose. "He's a bear all right," he told Marshall. "Dances just like one." Then he sniffed his hands and added, "Whee-oo. Smells like one too."

Everybody laughed. All except Melanie. While everyone else seemed to be having a great time, Melanie was looking more and more worried.

"What's the matter?" April whispered, pulling her aside, but almost before she finished asking, she began to guess.

"Marshall thinks that dog is really his," Melanie whispered back, which was almost exactly what April was guessing she would say.

April nodded. "Yeah, I was thinking of that. But you know what? The good news is he doesn't have any identification or even a license. I checked. He has a collar but no license tag. So maybe he is just a stray that doesn't belong to anybody."

"I know." Melanie's eyebrows had their worried tilt. "But we'll have to find out. We'll have to find out if some family in the neighborhood is missing a big black"—she smiled ruefully—"you know what."

"You know what—what?" Ken had obviously been eavesdropping. "What're you guys talking about? The end of the world or something?"

49

"No," April whispered, "she's just worried about how Marshall's going to take it if we find out that his 'bear' really belongs to someone else."

"Yeah, I thought of that." Ken actually seemed concerned. "Tough, huh?"

April and Melanie looked at Ken in surprise and then gave each other a look that said something like, "Well, what do you know. Ken Kamata being a nice guy? Big *surprise!*"

It wasn't so much of a surprise, though, when you thought about the fact that it was Marshall he was being nice about. Marshall seemed to have that kind of effect on people.

"Hey," Ken said suddenly, "we could check the bulletin board at Peterson's. If anybody in the neighborhood loses a pet, they usually put up a 'lost' notice there. We could look to see if anyone's advertising for a lost . . ." He stopped and grinned. "A lost—whatever. And then if there's no notice, we can just, you know, stop worrying about it."

Melanie sighed. "But I suppose we ought to put up our own 'found' notice, too. You know, the kind people put up when they've found somebody else's lost pet."

"Yeah, I suppose so," April said quickly. "I can do that. I'll be the one to do that, Melanie."

When Melanie looked at her sharply, April tried to look innocent. That was one of the problems about having such a close friend. The kind who guessed what you were thinking even when you didn't particularly want them to. Like when you were thinking that bulletin-board signs could be written in extremely small handwriting so that you'd practically have to have a microscope to read it. Or else it could be kind of crowded in underneath some of the other notices.

Melanie was still looking suspicious. "Anyway, even if nobody claims him, that still won't solve the whole problem. The rest of the problem is, Where is he going to live? It's against the rules at the Casa Rosada." She looked at Ken. "So I guess that kind of leaves it up to you or Toby."

" 'Fraid I can't help," Ken said. "My mom's allergic." He grinned. "She's allergic to dogs anyway, and I have a feeling that a bear would be just as bad. But maybe Toby could take him in. I'll bet he could. I know he and his dad used to have a dog a few years ago. Hey, Tobe. Come over here."

Toby stopped playing with Marshall and Bear and came over to the shed. "Yeah? What's up, Kamata?"

"We were talking about who should take Bear home with them." Ken grinned at Toby as he went on, "I guess the thing is the Casa Rosada has a strict rule about no bears, so that's out. And I can't because of my mom's allergies. So I guess that kind of leaves you."

At first Toby was smiling. "Yeah," he said, "I probably could. My dad doesn't mind having a . . ." But then, all of a sudden, his voice trailed off to nothing. "My dad doesn't . . . ," he repeated, and then for several seconds he didn't say anything at all. And when he did begin to talk, it was only to say, "No. I couldn't. Not right now. Not until . . . Well, probably not for a pretty long time."

When Toby said he couldn't take Bear home, it seemed to Melanie that he had a very un-Toby-like expression on his face. And even stranger was what he did when April and Ken started pestering him to tell them why he'd

51

changed his mind. And what was strangest of all was what he *didn't* do. Like not getting angry or even wising off. Instead, he just got a faraway look in his eyes, as if he was thinking about something so important he almost didn't hear them. And whatever he was thinking about wasn't making him feel very good.

Afterward April and Melanie remembered that the afternoon when Bear arrived was the first time they began to realize that Toby Alvillar was in some kind of trouble.

Nine

THE WAY IT actually turned out, Bear stayed all alone in the Gypsy Camp that night. Nobody liked the idea very much, particularly Marshall and Bear. But after Toby backed out of taking him home, there just wasn't any other solution. Everyone agreed that it had to be the Gypsy Camp or nothing. Everyone except Marshall, that is. Marshall kept insisting that they should at least ask Mr. Bodler.

"Maybe he'd say yes," Marshall kept saying. Mr. Bodler was the janitor at the Casa Rosada, as well as being the landlord's spy who tattled on anyone who broke the apartment-house rules. Rules like not having a dog. Marshall knew about the no dogs rule, but since he'd never heard of a no bears rule, he kept thinking Mr. Bodler just might say okay.

"I'm sure there must be a no bears rule too," Melanie told him, but that didn't convince Marshall. It wasn't until April said that she definitely remembered reading a no bears clause in Caroline's rental contract that Marshall gave up on asking the janitor and agreed to help make the old shed into a temporary bear shelter.

"Just till we figure out something better," Melanie told

him. "It's the only way. And you mustn't tell Mr. Bodler or anyone about him. If you do, they'll just come and take him away and put him in the pound."

"What's a pound?"

"It's a place where they put animals that nobody wants, and after a while if nobody comes for them, they have to kill them."

Marshall looked horrified. "I won't tell," he agreed. "Not ever." He patted Bear's shaggy head. "But what will he eat?"

"Good question, kid," April said. "Big question! Enough food for a bear that size is going to be a very big question." Then she looked around and added, "And the only answer has got to be—money!"

Immediately everyone looked at Ken. When money was the question, Ken was usually the answer. Sure enough, reaching into his pocket, Ken pulled out a whole fistful of coins and even a dollar bill or two. "Okay. I get the message," he said. "What should I get, Toby? What did you feed that dog you used to have? Hey, Tobe. I'm talking to you." Toby seemed to be spacing out again.

"Dog?" Marshall asked, frowning.

While Melanie explained to Marshall that bears and dogs eat pretty much the same kinds of things, Ken kept on trying to get Toby's attention. When he finally did, Toby said his dad used to feed their dog kibble.

Then, after Ken offered to go buy a bag of kibble, Toby kind of came back to earth and said he'd go along to help. And while they were at it, they could pick up an old baby-crib mattress that was part of his father's junk collection. A mattress that would be just the right size for a bear's bed.

"Won't your dad care if you take it?" Melanie asked.

"Naw, he probably won't even notice. Besides . . ." Toby stopped talking, and his eyes went unfocused again.

"Besides . . . ?" April prompted.

Toby shrugged. "Oh, nothing. I was just going to say that he's been trying to get rid of some of his junk lately. Taking stuff to the dump, and like that."

Melanie was puzzled. There wasn't anything scary about taking stuff to the dump. Particularly when you had as much of it as Toby's dad did. But there was definitely something about it that seemed to make Toby look—well, almost frightened.

So Toby and Ken went off together to get Bear a bed and something to eat, and Melanie went home to get a bunch of old raggedy blankets her mother was getting ready to throw away. Meanwhile April stayed in the storage yard with Marshall and Bear, but she didn't waste her time. While they waited, she cleaned out the sacred fire pit and made it into a bear-sized drinking bowl.

After Ken and Toby came staggering back carrying a baby-crib mattress and a huge sack of dog kibble, they all pitched in to help make the one-time Egyptian temple into a kind of international Bear hideout—Egyptian, Greek, American, and Gypsy. The secret hiding place for Egyptian hieroglyphic scrolls under the statue of the Greek goddess Diana became a storage place for a bag of American dog kibble, and the Gypsy caravan mural served as a great extra wall to make the bed more private and shield it from the wind. When they had finished, they stood around and watched Bear eat an amazing amount of kibble, drink from the sacred fire pit, tromp around in a circle on the crib mattress, and then lie down with his big black head resting on his paws. He looked pretty happy and contented right then, but when they all went out and locked the gate, he did whimper a little. And so did Marshall.

After the gate was locked, they all stood around for a moment and listened to the whimpering. "I sure hope he doesn't bark and bother the Professor," Melanie said, and when Marshall asked, "Do bears bark?" everyone kind of sighed and ignored him. It was late by then and getting dark, and nobody had the energy to deal with any more bear versus dog debates.

They'd started down the alley next to the Casa Rosada when Ken looked at his watch and said, "*Sheesh*. I didn't know it was so late. I got to get home. So long, everybody. So long . . ." He looked around. "Hey, where's Alvillar?"

It wasn't until then that they noticed that Toby was gone. He'd apparently taken off for home as soon as they left the Gypsy Camp without waiting to say good-bye to anybody. Not even Ken. Which was another definitely un-Toby-like action. On the way up the stairs at the Casa Rosada, April wanted to bring up the subject, but Melanie was busy reminding Marshall that he wasn't to tell anybody about Bear.

"Not anybody!" she said again pointedly. "At least not yet."

Marshall got the message. "Not even Mom and Dad," he said. "Not yet. Or the pound will get him. . . ."

"Right!" Melanie said. They'd reached the door to the Rosses' apartment by then, and as soon as Marshall disappeared inside, Melanie turned to April and said just what

April had been thinking of saying, "What do you suppose is wrong with Toby? He was acting kind of weird today, don't you think?"

"That's just what I was going to ask you," April said.

They made a couple of guesses then, like maybe he and his father really were starving, or maybe his father was sick. But neither one seemed too likely.

"He'd have told us if it was anything like that," Melanie said. "Or told Ken, anyway. It must be something else."

"Yeah," April agreed. "Something more . . ."

"*Mysterious*," they said in unison.

The next morning April got up early and made her own breakfast. Then, still sitting at the kitchen table, she began to work on the "found" notice for Peterson's bulletin board. Written on a torn piece of notebook paper, in tiny, almost unreadable handwriting, the notice said: FOUND: *One large black shaggy-haired dog. Please call 555-6790.* Not that her handwriting was ever the greatest, but this time she had taken special pains to make it illegible. Just as she finished checking to see if it needed any more smears or scribbles, the kitchen door opened and her grandmother came in.

Caroline was dressed for work in one of her boring business suits, and her gray hair was pinned back in its usual neat bun. The way she dressed had been one of the reasons April had been sure her grandmother was going to be a real drag. At least she'd thought that at first, before they'd had a chance to get better acquainted.

"Hey," April said, quickly putting the "found" notice in her pocket. "I thought you weren't working today."

"I thought so too," Caroline said. "But I'm having to fill in on short notice. And I'm running late." As she hurriedly started the coffee and put some bread in the toaster, she told April that she'd already checked with Mrs. Ross and it would be the usual arrangement for workdays when school was out. The usual arrangement was that April had lunch with the Rosses and during the rest of the day at least checked in with Mrs. Ross from time to time. Which turned out to be pretty automatic anyway, since she and Melanie Ross were generally together.

"Some toast?" Caroline asked April as she poured the coffee.

April shook her head. "No thanks. I got up early and fixed my own breakfast."

"Oh, did you?" Caroline stopped bustling around long enough to give her a surprised look. "Something special going on in Egypt today?" she asked.

"Not Egypt," April said, grinning. "Remember? It's the Gypsy Camp now."

"That's right, you did tell me. I was forgetting. And you were about to introduce Ken to the change of scene." She mugged an exaggeratedly anxious face. "Well, how did it go?"

But April barely got started telling her when she had to rush off to work. "I'll have to hear all about it tonight," she said over her shoulder.

"Yeah," April called after her, "tonight. I'll tell you all about it tonight." And the strange thing was, she probably would. While April cleared off the breakfast dishes and put on her backpack, she was thinking about how it still seemed a little weird to be telling an adult about stuff like the Gypsy Camp. But Caroline was different. You could tell Caroline anything. Well, almost anything, she corrected herself, as she pulled the "found" notice out of her pocket to check it one last time.

Ten

NOT LONG AFTER her grandmother left for work, April left the Casa Rosada too, and headed down Orchard Avenue for Peterson's grocery store. It had seemed strange passing the door to the Rosses' apartment without stopping to see if Melanie could go too. Particularly since Melanie was the one who'd insisted that they should post a "found" notice in the first place. But Melanie had this thing about being fair, and she just might think it wasn't fair to post a "found" notice that nobody would ever see. And probably couldn't read even if they did see it. So for just this once April decided to go alone.

Peterson's was a small neighborhood grocery that did a lot of community-type services like delivering food to old people and keeping a bulletin board in the entryway where customers could post notices about things such as rentals and jobs and things for sale. One corner of the board was marked off to be used just for "Lost and Found." Before pinning up her own note, April inspected the board carefully.

There were, as usual, two or three missing cats, plus a found cockatiel—and one very large poster about a lost dog. April studied the dog poster carefully before she breathed a sigh of relief. The dog was described as white with black spots and weighing about twenty-five pounds. Definitely not Bear. The other good thing about the lost dog was the size of its notice, which meant that there really wasn't room for anything new except, of course, directly under some other things. Which would be pretty frustrating if you were desperate to have lots of people read what you'd written, but wasn't any problem if you weren't. April smiled smugly as she tacked up her notice—directly under one of the cats and a part of the lost dog. She was just stepping back to see if anything was showing that shouldn't be when Toby Alvillar came out of the store.

Toby was carrying a big paper bag and a mop, and he seemed to be in a hurry, but when he saw April, he slid to a stop.

"Hey, what do you know. It's February." He did one of his crazy eye rolls that meant he was about to make a joke. "I thought it was still December, but now here it is February already. How time flies!"

"Very funny," April said in a disgusted tone of voice. Then, remembering how Toby had mysteriously disappeared the night before, she asked, "Hey, where'd you go last night, after we left"—she lowered her voice—"the Gypsy Camp? You were there one minute and then you weren't, and nobody saw you go. Ken was looking for you."

Suddenly the stand-up comedian was gone and the worried, spacey look was back on Toby's face. "Yeah," he said, "I just had to—get home. I had to find out . . ." His grin came back, but somehow it didn't seem real. "I just remembered something I had to find out."

"Find out?" April prompted. Toby didn't take the bait,

61

so she tried another question. "Hey, what's with the big mop?"

"Yeah"—Toby seemed glad to change the subject— "some mop, isn't it. First one we've had in about six years. I wore out the last one when I was in kindergarten."

That sounded like another of Toby's tall tales. "Gimme a break," April said. "I'll bet you never mopped a floor in your life."

Toby laughed. "Not mopping," he said. "You know, riding the range." He straddled the mop handle and started galloping in circles, yelling, "Ride 'em, cowboy!"

April was trying to keep from laughing when Toby's mop-headed mustang tripped and he dropped his paper bag, scattering all sorts of cleaning stuff across the sidewalk. As she helped gather up S.O.S. pads, cleanser, scrub brushes, and several kinds of soaps and disinfectants, she said, "Looks like somebody's going to be doing some housecleaning." Remembering what the Alvillar attic looked like, she thought of adding that it was about time, but she managed to control herself. Instead, she said, "Hey, you guys going to have a party or something? Bet you're getting ready for a big New Year's Eve party."

But Toby's tense, anxious expression had come back. "No party," he started to say, shaking his head slowly. Then suddenly he was the old Toby again. "Yeah, that's it. A party. My dad's having this big blast tonight for a bunch of his friends. So we've got to shine the old place up a little."

April wanted to ask some more questions about the party, but everything was back in the bag by then, and suddenly Toby took off running. Clutching the bag and mop, he disappeared around the corner toward University Avenue, without even waiting to say good-bye. April watched until he was out of sight before she started home.

April was back on Orchard Avenue and still wondering about Toby when, just as she passed the A–Z Store, she happened to see the Professor. She had been noticing the store's clean windows at the time and the artistic way the junk and antiques were arranged now that Elizabeth's mom was working there. The windows were so clean, in fact, that she could see the Professor himself, sitting at his desk at the rear of the store. On the spur of the moment she decided it would be a good idea to talk to him. Partly just for a visit, but also to find out if the Professor might have seen anything strange in his storage yard last night. Or heard any unusual noises, like a barking dog, for instance. If there had been a problem, she decided, it would be best if she and Melanie found out about it before the Professor did something drastic, like calling the police, or maybe the pound.

The Professor was working on his account books, but when April came in, he seemed really glad to see her. Dr. Julian Huddleston—the Professor's real name—was as thin and bent as ever, and his dark, deep-set eyes still looked a bit mysterious. But now, instead of being blank and empty, they had a lively, curious gleam. Curious, in particular, about anything April had to say.

"Well, good morning, Miss Hall," he said. "And what new enterprise are you pursuing on this beautiful last day of the year?" Even though the Professor's rating had gone way up on the friendliness scale, his conversation still tended to be a little bit on the stuffy side. April said she was fine and wished him a Happy New Year. They went on chatting about whether the beautiful weather was going to last for New Year's Day before she got around to mentioning the storage yard and the Land of Egypt. She didn't call it the Gypsy Camp because she really didn't have time to go into the reasons for the change right at the moment. And besides, she certainly didn't want to make the Professor think that he'd see anything new and interesting if he looked out his rear window. Like something new and interesting and covered with shaggy black hair, for instance.

Instead, she just said that no one had been spending much time in Egypt because of all the holiday trips and visits, but that they all had been there again just yesterday. "All of us," she told him. "Did you hear us yesterday? There wasn't too much noise, was there, like in the evening?"

The Professor said he hadn't heard any unusual noises the evening before, which was a big relief. After visiting for a few more minutes, April asked if she could look around before she went home, "Just to see if you have any new ancient things," she said. But what she really wanted to see was how easy it would be for the Professor to see through the window in his back room nowadays, the window that looked right into what had once been his storage yard, before it became the Land of Egypt, and was at present the Gypsy Camp. Not to mention, and she certainly didn't intend to, the temporary home of a large, shaggy animal.

Back in the old days before Mrs. Chung took over, the rear window had been almost too dirty to see through, but things were a lot cleaner now, which might present a problem. So April snooped around for a few minutes before she headed back to the Casa Rosada feeling very relieved. As soon as she got to the Rosses' apartment, she started telling Melanie all about everything—the good news and the not so good. The good news about how she had posted the "found dog" notice and how the Professor couldn't even get near his rear window anytime soon, because the back room was so crowded with new merchandise. And the not-so-good news about running into Toby and how he still seemed to be in a pretty weird mood.

But on that particular morning telling Melanie anything the least bit private wasn't easy. Mrs. Ross was home, and both Marshall and Melanie had chores to do. So April had to follow Melanie around while she vacuumed, while Marshall followed them both around dragging a bunch of toys he was supposed to be picking up and whining that he wanted to go see Bear.

"Come on, Melanie," he kept whimpering, "I got to go see my Bear. Right now."

"Shhh," Melanie kept saying, "Mom will hear you." But he kept right on. Once or twice April was pretty sure his mom did hear him, but she didn't seem to pay any attention. April guessed that she figured Bear was just one more of Marshall's imaginary animals.

April was still screeching away about Toby, trying to be heard over the roar of the vacuum, when Melanie suddenly turned off the switch.

"Like he was what?"

"Like he was"—April toned her screech down to a whisper in midsentence—"nervous. Scared almost."

"Yeah, scared. That's what I thought yesterday. Scared."

Melanie nodded slowly, her forehead puckered into a worried frown. Then she turned on the switch and went back across the room. And April went on following her, feeling very frustrated. She hated having to compete with a vacuum and a whining kid when she had important things to talk about.

By the time the Ross kids finished all their chores and received permission to go outside for one hour, Marshall was practically standing on his head with impatience. When April and Melanie got out onto the landing, he was already tearing down the stairs, with his shoes untied and his jacket only halfway on. And *no* Security. Melanie pointed that out right away. "Look, April. No Security. And this time, *don't* mention it."

April promised she wouldn't.

They didn't stop by for Elizabeth because the Chungs were still away visiting relatives, so it was only a few minutes later that they reached the gate to the Gypsy Camp and were almost trampled and kissed to death by a wildly joyful Bear.

"A bouncing Bear," Melanie said, a few minutes later. She and April were sitting on the edge of the shed floor watching as Bear bounced around the yard with Marshall right behind him.

"Yeah. And a bouncing Marshall, too," April said. "Marshall seems—different. You know, when he's around Bear."

"Different?" Melanie asked. "How different?"

April couldn't put her finger on it at first. "Well, kind of . . . Well, like he was younger. Not so—dignified."

Melanie understood right away. "Yeah. Right!" she said. "More like your normal pain-in-the-neck four-year-old."

They'd talked before, lots of times, about how dignified and grown-up Marshall was, almost like he didn't know how to be a little kid. Except where Security was concerned, of course. But now suddenly, it was as if he didn't need to be so grown-up, or need Security so much either. And it seemed to be Bear that made the difference, which was pretty amazing.

Bear was amazing in other ways, too. April had never had a dog before, and neither had the Rosses, so they were all surprised to find out how smart he was. For instance, he knew that his bag of kibble was hidden in the base of the statue of Diana, and he knew how to make it very clear that he wanted them to get some out. He knew how to let them know he wanted to play tug-of-war with one of his blankets, and he also knew how to walk on his hind legs even without anyone holding up his front paws. And, as Melanie pointed out, he was careful to poop neatly only in one corner of the yard. It was the kind of thing that an organized person like Melanie would be sure to notice.

No one else showed up at the Gypsy Camp that day, but April and Melanie weren't too surprised. Toby was probably too busy cleaning house, and who knew what Ken was doing.

"He's probably home getting ready for a party too," Melanie said. "The Kamatas have lots of parties." They waited around a little longer, but no one came, so they fed Bear one more time and went on home.

New Year's Eve was pretty quiet at the Halls' that night.

67

After dinner April was in her room reading when she began to hear the sound of firecrackers and horns, and right afterward the phone rang and it was Melanie.

"Hi." Melanie sounded worried. "I hear loud noises. Outside I mean."

"Big news," April said sarcastically. "Loud noises? On New Year's Eve? I can't believe it."

"I know." Melanie paused and then went on, "I know it's New Year's Eve. But I didn't hear any *dogs* barking, though. You know, some *dogs* bark like crazy when they hear loud noises. Particularly when they hear the kind of loud noises like on New Year's Eve."

"Oh yeah. I get it." April said, and she really did. What she got was that Melanie was trying to tell her something without actually saying it. Like maybe she was in the same room with her parents or something. "Okay," April said, "I'll go out on the balcony and check." They went on talking for a few minutes, wishing each other Happy New Year, to make it sound like a normal conversation, before they hung up and April hurried out to the balcony.

Since the balcony of Caroline's apartment was on the A–Z side of the Casa Rosada, it was a good place to listen for noises that might be coming from the storage yard. But there weren't any. The Gypsy Camp seemed to be very quiet. It was such a beautiful night, strangely warm for New Year's Eve, that April stayed out on the balcony for longer than she'd meant to. When she finally came in and called Melanie, Mrs. Ross answered the phone.

"Oh, hi, Mrs. Ross," April said. "I just called to tell Melanie . . . That is, I just called to wish her a Happy New Year."

Mrs. Ross laughed. "Melanie just went to bed. Besides, I was under the impression that you girls covered the New Year's wishes thing pretty thoroughly just a few minutes ago."

"Well, yes, we did, k-k-kind of," April stammered. "It's just that I remembered something I forgot to tell Melanie. I forgot to say that it was a very *quiet* New Year's Eve. Very *quiet*. Would you please tell Melanie that?"

Mrs. Ross sounded puzzled, but she said she would.

Eleven

ON NEW YEAR'S DAY morning April and Caroline had just finished watching the Rose Parade and were having lunch when the phone rang. It was Melanie.

"Hi," she said. "I guess Marshall and I are going to the Gypsy Camp. Want to come?"

"Right this minute?"

"Yes. Or as soon as you can, at least. It's Marshall. He's been bugging me to go see . . ." Her voice dropped to a whisper. "It's the Bear thing again. He wants to see Bear."

"Well, we're having lunch."

"I know." Melanie sounded exasperated. "We just finished. But Marshall keeps fussing at me. And Mom said we could go. She and Dad are going to watch the game."

So April gulped down the rest of her lunch and ran down to the second floor. Marshall was waiting outside the Rosses' door. Without Security again. On the way down the stairs April whispered to Melanie that it was beginning to look as if bears had just about pushed octopuses clear off Marshall's personal-best list. And Melanie said she thought so, too.

It was that morning, as soon as they reached the Gypsy Camp and Bear was jumping all over them as usual, that the subject of a bath came up. Actually, it was Melanie who suggested it. Melanie, as April had noticed before, had a couple of serious hang-ups. Like being fair, for instance. And right next to being fair, Melanie was hung up on being clean. And when you got anywhere near Bear, it was pretty obvious that he wasn't. Clean, that is. Actually, it didn't bother April all that much. As far as she was concerned, Bear just had a smell that you might call normally doggy, but Melanie didn't agree. According to Melanie, Bear's smell was worse than normal, and they ought to do something about it. It didn't take her long to have a plan all worked out.

"That hose by the back of the store would reach if we bring it in under the fence, and I could go home for some shampoo, and we could give him a good scrubbing," she said. "It would be good for him."

"No, it's too cold," Marshall said. "And bears hate to take baths."

Melanie giggled. "How do you know? How do you know that bears hate to take baths, just because you do?"

"I know." Marshall frowned fiercely. "They hate it. Bear told me."

April laughed, but she couldn't help being a little bit on Marshall's side. Even though it was a warm morning for New Year's Day, it didn't seem warm enough to make an outdoor bath with cold water very much fun. So it was two against one, and Melanie was about to give up on the idea when Ken Kamata suddenly burst through the gate. His face was flushed, and he seemed to be breathing hard as if he'd run a long way.

"Hey, Kamata. What's up?" April said.

Ken looked around. "Is Tobe here?" he asked.

71

April made a gesture that meant it was pretty obvious that he wasn't.

"Yeah, I guess not." Ken took a deep breath and then shrugged. "Okay," he said, "so what's up with you? What are you guys doing?"

So they told him. All about the bath argument and who had been on which side and why.

"Yeah, I guess it is pretty cold for an outdoor bath," he said.

"You could help us," Melanie said. "If you helped, we'd get done faster."

For a second or two it looked as if Ken might be going to say yes. "Well," he said, "I guess I could . . ." But then he shook his head. "No. I've got to get right home. I'm trying to find . . . That is, I'm kind of—I'm expecting a phone call." He thought for a minute before he added, "Hey. You could bathe him at our house."

April and Melanie were amazed. "At your house?" April asked. "But I thought you said your mom was allergic."

"She is. But she's working at my dad's office right now." He grinned and added, "All day. They always work all day on New Year's getting the books all up-to-date. My dad says it's a Kamata tradition." He stood back and studied Bear thoughtfully before he nodded. "Yeah, I think he'd fit. See, there's this extra-big stationary tub in my mom's laundry room."

The next question was how they were going to get clear to the Kamatas' house without being seen by anyone they knew. At least by anyone who knew them well enough to ask embarrassing questions like whose dog was that and where did they get it. But then Ken pointed out that they could stay in the alleys as far as Norwich Avenue and then cut across the vacant lot to Elm. "And you're almost there," he finished.

After that there was only the problem of a leash, which Melanie solved by offering to go home for a long skinny piece of jump rope.

While Melanie was gone, Ken decided to run home by himself. He said it was just so he could get the laundry room ready, but April had a feeling he didn't want to risk being seen by anyone he knew. He was just plain panic-stricken that one of his macho-type sixth-grade buddies would see him walking with two girls, a little kid, and a weird-looking dog. All she said was, "Okay. See you there in a few minutes." She thought about adding, "You chicken!" but at the last moment she decided against it.

So Ken took off down the alley, and April kept an eye on Marshall and Bear and congratulated herself on getting better at making last-minute decisions not to say stupid things. It wasn't long before Melanie showed up with the rope and a big bottle of Marshall's baby shampoo.

The laundry room at the Kamatas' was pretty impressive. Like the rest of the house, it was extra-large and equipped with all the latest stuff. The stationary tub was definitely king-sized, and Ken really had gotten things ready. There was a big bunch of beach towels stacked on the dryer, and Ken was already running the water when the rest of them came in the back door. So the bath was ready for Bear, but it soon became obvious Bear wasn't ready for a bath. Not if he could help it, anyway.

Judging by the smell, you might have thought that Bear had never had a bath before, but apparently he had. At least, when he heard the water running, he seemed to know exactly what was about to happen. And Marshall had been right when he said that Bear would hate it. As soon as Ken shut off the faucet and turned toward Bear, he began to whine and back away. And when Ken said, "Okay, boy, it's all ready. Jump in," Bear flopped down on his back with all four feet in the air.

So getting Bear into the tub turned out to be a really high-risk project. Not that he ever growled or threatened to bite. He just went limp and refused to cooperate. It took all four of them pulling and pushing to stand him up and shove him toward the tub. Then, when Ken put Bear's front paws on the edge of the tub, his hind legs collapsed and he sat down. And when Ken pulled up on Bear's rear end, his front paws came down off the tub. It went on like that for quite a while, with April and Melanie having fits of hysterics and Ken laughing too, now and then, in between saying, *"Sheesh!"* under his breath and some other pretty gross-sounding things in Japanese that he refused to translate.

Finally, with April and Melanie lifting on each side and with Ken at the rear, they got Bear into the tub, and suddenly the battle seemed to be over. Once he was in the water, he just stood there looking quietly miserable while Ken held his head and the girls soaped him up. With all that long black fur, it took half a bottle of baby shampoo and lots of scrubbing before he was completely covered with white suds.

"Hey, look!" Melanie said. "Now he's a polar bear."

"Yeah, maybe," April said. "A polar bear with black roots."

Ken didn't say anything. In fact, he'd been strangely quiet ever since the bath had started. Quiet and preoccupied, as if he was waiting and listening for something to happen. But then, when they'd almost finished rinsing off the suds, Ken suddenly yelled, "There it is! There's the phone," released his hold on Bear's head, and disappeared through the kitchen door. And of course the minute his head was free, Bear jumped out of the tub and . . .

"Look out!" April yelled, and started to run for cover, but it was too late. Bear shook himself.

Ken was in the kitchen a long time. While he was gone, April and Melanie got most of the flood cleaned up. By using up at least half a dozen beach towels, they'd gotten Marshall and Bear and the laundry room at least partly dry, and they'd started in on drying each other when Ken finally came back. April's blond hair was straggling in wet strings around her face, water and suds were still dripping off Melanie's chin, and they were both having fits of hysterical laughter. But when they saw Ken's face, they quit laughing.

For a moment no one said anything. Then April swallowed hard and asked, "What is it? What's wrong?"

Ken's shoulders lifted in a strange, jerky shrug. "I don't know. I don't . . ." His voice faded out to a whisper and then came back again. "It's Toby. Toby is—gone."

Twelve

"GONE?" APRIL FINALLY managed to ask. "What do you mean, 'gone'? Gone where?"

Ken shook his head. "I don't know. His dad doesn't know. That was Tobe's dad on the phone. What he said was Toby went to bed last night, and this morning—" Ken gulped, blinked, and then went on, "And this morning, he wasn't there."

Silence. Marshall came over and grabbed his sister's arm the way he always did when he was frightened, and even Bear seemed to realize that something was terribly wrong. He'd been jumping around like crazy, celebrating the end of his bath, but suddenly he stopped prancing and lay down with his chin on his front paws.

At last Melanie said, "But he can't be gone. April saw him just yesterday morning. Didn't you, April?"

April nodded. "Yesterday morning. At Peterson's." She thought for a moment. "Maybe it has something to do with the party. He said his dad was going to have a big party. He was buying a mop and some other stuff to get ready for it."

"A party?" Ken's forehead wrinkled. "Toby's dad didn't say anything about a party. He did say some people were there to see them yesterday afternoon, but it didn't sound like any party."

"Hmmm," April said. "Maybe his dad was lying. Maybe there really was a party last night, and his dad got so smashed he doesn't know what happened. And maybe something happened at the party that . . ." Her voice trailed away into silence, but her mind was still going, bringing up all the stories her mom and stepfather used to tell about Hollywood parties they'd been to or heard about. Stories about people who got smashed or OD'd on drugs and . . .

"About the visitors they had yesterday?" Melanie asked Ken. "Who were they? Do you think they might have had something to do with it?"

"I don't think so." Ken shook his head. "Andre, that's Toby's father, said that he'd already called them this morning, and they said they haven't seen Toby either."

"But who were they?" April's mind was still working overtime, bringing up scenes from the hundreds of scary movies she used to see before she came to live with Caroline. Movies that came on TV late at night when her mom was out singing with a band. She could remember lots of scenes in which scary visitors played a part. Visitors who didn't knock and who came in with guns or knives and . . .

"They were—the visitors were . . . ," Ken said, but then he shook his head. "I can't talk about it. I promised Toby I wouldn't tell anyone about them."

And that was absolutely all Ken would say. Except that he'd called Toby that morning, and his father had answered.

"He sounded kind of frantic," Ken said, "but he didn't say Toby had disappeared or anything. Not then, anyway. Just that he wasn't there. He said he'd tell Tobe to call me as soon as he found him. But I could tell by his voice that something was wrong. I mean *really* wrong. And just now when he called, he said that Toby had—disappeared."

That was all they could get Ken to say. When they tried again to bring up the subject of the Alvillars' visitors, he just shook his head.

"I guess you guys might as well go on home," he said. "I've got to go to my dad's office. I've got to tell them about Toby. I mean, I don't know what else to do. Maybe they'll think of something."

So April, Melanie, Marshall, and Bear, of course, started back to the Gypsy Camp. On the way they walked quietly and fast, glancing behind trash containers and down side streets as if they expected something dangerous to be lying in wait just out of sight. The kind of danger that might make someone go to bed at night and disappear before morning.

Nothing unusual happened on the way, but they'd only been back in the Gypsy Camp for a few minutes when something scary did happen. Bear had gone back to his bed behind the painting of the caravan and the rest of them were sitting along the edge of the shed floor talking softly when someone or something started trying to get in.

When the Professor had the new lock put on the gate to the storage yard, he'd also added a dead-bolt latch on the inside so that people who belonged inside could keep uninvited people from coming in. It hadn't been used much—up until now. But as soon as they had entered the yard,

Melanie had quickly and firmly closed the latch. And now, suddenly, it started to jiggle.

Except for one short, soft woofing noise from Bear, no one said a thing. Absolutely silent and motionless, they watched and listened while the rattling went on and on and then . . .

"Melanie," a soft voice said. "April. Are you in there?" April poked Melanie's arm and managed a slightly wobbly smile. They should have known. It was only Elizabeth. Melanie ran to open the latch.

"Hi, Bethy," Melanie said weakly. Elizabeth was wearing a new quilted jacket, her hair was tied back in the style that made her into a Queen Nefertiti look-alike, and she was smiling happily.

"Hi, everybody. We just got home from San Francisco. Hi, Melanie. Your mom said you were here, so I came right on—" She stopped in midsentence, gasped, and whispered, "What's wrong?"

Melanie gave April a warning look. A look that reminded her how sensitive Elizabeth was and how she could come completely unglued over things that were a lot less serious than whatever it was that had happened to Toby. April got the message. But while they were still thinking of the best way to put it, Elizabeth gasped again. Gasped and pointed at the back of the shed where Bear was emerging from behind the Gypsy caravan. "What's—what's that?"

Marshall jumped up and threw his arms around Bear's neck. "He's Bear," he said. "My Bear."

For once April didn't mind the interruption. Explaining Bear was a lot easier than explaining—some other things. She did the short version. Just the part about how Bear had

79

showed up and how Marshall had recognized him immediately as his *Bear* and how they hadn't told any non-Gypsies about him yet. Not until they'd had time to figure out how to keep him from being sent to the pound. And how, meanwhile, he was going to stay in the Gypsy Camp. Then Elizabeth, who was usually a little afraid of large animals, came over timidly to say hello. And Bear, who seemed to understand the situation immediately, greeted her gently with only a small bounce or two and a few friendly licks. Elizabeth was obviously thrilled to death.

"He's so big. But he's not a bit scary," she said. "And he smells so good."

April and Melanie would have cracked up if it weren't for their other news. "But there's something else we have to tell you," April said reluctantly. "It's about Toby."

Telling Elizabeth that Toby had disappeared wasn't easy. She started sobbing almost immediately, and when they finally finished, it took another ten minutes to calm her down from positively hysterical to occasional sniffles and hiccups.

"Look, don't worry about it," Melanie told Elizabeth as they climbed up the front steps at the Casa Rosada. "I think Toby probably just had a fight with his father and ran away. He'll probably show up tomorrow."

"Yeah," April said. "That's probably all it is."

"*Ran away,*" Elizabeth said, and started to cry all over again.

So they sat down on the steps and waited, and after a while Elizabeth stopped sobbing enough to ask, "Can I tell my mom?"

April and Melanie consulted each other with a look and

then both nodded. "Sure," April said. "We're going to tell our folks about it. I've got a feeling that even if we didn't, they'd be hearing about it real soon anyhow."

April was right about that. It wasn't long before practically everybody had heard about Toby's disappearance. The first ones to hear were Caroline and the Rosses and Mrs. Chung and right after that the telephoning started. The Rosses called Caroline, and Mrs. Chung called the Rosses, and apparently almost everybody called the Kamatas. So it wasn't until the adults finally got off the phone that April was able to talk to Melanie again.

"Hi," April began. "What's happening? Your phone's been busy for hours. Did your folks find out anything? Have they found Toby yet?"

"No. I guess not," Melanie said. "Not yet. All I know is that everybody is really worried. And my folks tried to call Toby's dad, but he won't talk to anybody. He said he wants to keep the line open in case Toby calls. But my dad thinks he just doesn't want to answer too many questions."

So a lot of people knew about Toby's disappearance before they went to bed that night, and a lot more heard about it for the first time from the principal at school the next day. There was the usual back-to-school assembly where Mr. Adams, the principal, welcomed everyone back from their holiday vacation. But this time, as soon as he'd done the welcoming, Mr. Adams told the whole school that Toby Alvillar was missing. He didn't give any details. Just that Toby Alvillar was gone, and if anyone knew anything about where he might be, they were to come to the office immediately. Mr. Adams also said, "If you are one of Toby's special friends, you might be called in later, even if

81

you don't think you know anything, just to have a little talk with me and some other people." Other people who, according to rumor, were probably the police.

At the first recess April and Melanie talked about what might happen. Everyone knew that Ken and Toby were best friends, so Ken would certainly be called in. But since the Egypt and Gypsy Games had always been pretty much of a secret, at least at school, Ken might be the only one.

"I sure hope they don't call me in," Melanie said.

"Me too," April agreed. But in a way, she almost wished they would. She really wanted to find out what the police knew. If they called her into the principal's office, a lot of questions were going to be asked, and she was planning to do some of the asking. Back in the sixth-grade classroom she was still thinking about the things she wanted to bring up when the speaker buzzed and Mr. Adams's voice asked for Ken Kamata to be sent to the office.

Ken went out looking nervous and self-conscious, and in exactly fifteen minutes and ten seconds—April was timing him—he came back looking pretty much the same. April was craning her neck trying to get a look at Ken's face when the buzzer went off again. This time the call was for April Hall.

It took her a split second to sort through excitement, curiosity, and apprehension and come up with her famous deadpan, before she walked out of the room, carefully not noticing how many people were staring after her.

Actually, the people in the principal's office were kind of a disappointment. Not that she'd been expecting Sherlock Holmes and Dr. Watson exactly, but when it turned out to be just Mr. Adams and two ordinary-looking, middle-aged women, it was kind of a letdown. Particularly when all they asked about was the mood Toby had seemed to be in when she'd seen him at Peterson's grocery store. But April made the best of it, especially when she got back to the classroom and everyone started asking her questions.

Thirteen

"HOW MANY?" April repeated when people asked her how many detectives had been waiting in the principal's office. "Well, there were just these three people in there. I'm not sure how many of them were detectives." And when they asked her what the third degree was like, all she said was, "It was pretty scary, but I can't talk about it now. They made me promise I wouldn't." That was absolutely the truth, at least the part about promising not to talk. The two women, who might have been school psychologists, hadn't been particularly scary. The only scary part had been how worried all three of them seemed to be about what might have happened to Toby.

That's what April told Melanie on their way home from school that afternoon. They'd stopped at the day-care center to pick up Marshall, and at the moment he was walking a few feet ahead of them, talking with Elizabeth. That is, Marshall was talking, about Bear probably, and Elizabeth was listening, which made it easier for April and Melanie to talk about the Toby thing without anybody getting hysterical.

April had told Melanie all about the interview in the principal's office. That didn't count as breaking her promise, April explained, because nobody, not even school psychologists, expected a person to keep secrets from her best friend. "They said Toby probably just ran away, but they seemed awfully worried. Like maybe they didn't want to tell me what they really think." Melanie nodded, looking worried and frightened. Not hysterical. Melanie didn't get hysterical. But definitely frightened.

When they got to the Gypsy Camp, Ken was already there waiting. He started to talk about Toby right away, but Melanie shook her head and pointed to Marshall.

"Why?" Ken asked. "He was there yesterday, in the laundry room. So he knows about it."

Melanie nodded. "Right. He knows. But he doesn't always remember about it. Like right now, for instance." She pointed to where Bear and Marshall were bouncing around the yard.

"Yeah. I see what you mean," Ken said.

They all stood around for a few minutes and watched Bear and Marshall play tug-of-war with the rope leash before Melanie said, "We can't stay long. If we're late getting home today, it will be nine-one-one time." She made a frantic face and pretended to punch phone buttons.

"Yeah, me too." Ken looked disgusted. "Everybody's hitting the panic button *again*."

They all nodded. They knew what Ken meant by that "again." That all the adults were remembering Mr. Schmitt's cousin and what had almost happened to April back in November. They all looked at April. "Yeah," she said, trying not to sound pleased with the extra attention. "But that's dumb because—"

"Right. Real dumb," Ken interrupted. April glared at him, but he went right on, "because that red-haired guy is locked up now, and besides the police don't really suspect foul play." Ken was looking even more self-important than usual.

"Did the police tell you that when you were in the office?" April asked.

"The police?" Ken said. "Those two women in Mr. Adams's office weren't police. One of them was a psychologist, and I don't know who the other one was. The one who kept taking notes. And what they told me was that they think Tobe probably just—"

"Ran away," April interrupted. "That's what they told me, too. But maybe that's not what they really believe. I'll bet they're just telling us kids that so we won't panic. Anyway I asked them lots of questions, and they said they think he just decided to run away."

"Do *you* think Toby ran away?" Elizabeth asked Ken. "Why would he do that?"

Ken shook his head. "I don't know."

"Do you think he was mad at his father?" Melanie asked.

"Yeah," April agreed, "I was wondering that, too. I mean, Toby's dad doesn't exactly seem like your typical ideal father figure. Like, maybe he kind of takes it out on Toby because nobody wants to buy his weird piles of junk."

"No." Ken shook his head harder. "I don't think that was the reason."

"Then how about those visitors?" Melanie asked. "You know, you said there were some visitors the afternoon before Toby disappeared. Could they have something to do with it?"

"I told you." Ken glared at Melanie. "I promised I wouldn't talk about them."

Ken was still frowning and shaking his head when a familiar voice, which seemed to be coming from someplace very near, said, "That's all right, Ken. You can tell them now."

For a split second everyone looked around frantically, checking to see if everyone else had heard it too, or if it had only been their own private hallucination. Then they all turned back to where—to where Toby Alvillar was strolling nonchalantly out from behind the Gypsy caravan mural.

"Hi, guys," Toby said. "What's up?"

A moment's stunned surprise—and they all pounced on him. Ken was pounding him on the back, and everybody was pounding him with questions. Questions like, "Where have you been?" "Why did you run away?" and "What do you think you're doing, Alvillar, scaring everybody half to death?" And "*Sheesh*, Tobe. You weren't kidnapped, were you? Some people thought you were kidnapped."

Even Marshall had a question. "Why were you sleeping in Bear's bed?"

Toby sat down on the edge of the shed floor, and Bear came over and put his head in his lap. Scratching behind Bear's ears, Toby looked around at all the staring eyes, grinned, nodded, and answered Marshall's question first. "What was I doing in Bear's bed? Well, actually I was sleeping, till you guys barged in and woke me up. First sleep I've had in three days."

Marshall nodded thoughtfully and wandered off to disappear behind the mural, and Toby began to answer the other questions. "No, I wasn't kidnapped. Not exactly. But I would have been if I hadn't run away."

Somebody gasped, probably Elizabeth.

"Yeah, that's right," Toby went on. "I ran away to keep from being kidnapped."

Everyone asked questions at once. "By whom?" Melanie's voice was tense and quick, but April's was cool and suspicious. "Who would want to kidnap you, Alvillar?"

Toby stopped scratching Bear's ears and began scratching his own ankles. Both of them. "Fleas," he explained. "I'm afraid our Gypsy Bear has fleas." Lowering his voice, he added, "Plain old American dog fleas, as far as I can tell."

"We just bathed him yesterday," April said indignantly.

"Yeah, I could tell"—Toby grinned—"and was I ever glad. He smells great now. Even his fleas smell great."

"But about the kidnappers," Ken insisted. "What about them?"

"Oh yeah. Well, see . . ." Toby paused and thought before he went on, "see, a month or so ago these people showed up at our place and said they were my grandparents and . . ."

"Hey," Ken said. "You told me not to tell about that. You made me promise on my word of honor not to mention—"

"I know, and you were great. You were really hanging in there about not telling. But the thing is, I've decided now that I'd better come clean. I mean, let you guys in on the big secret. See, it's kind of a long story, but . . ." Toby paused again, sighed, and began: "The thing is, it turned out these people, who said they were my mother's parents—"

"Wait a minute!" April interrupted. "You said you never had a mother. Like you just came out of a test tube, or something."

Then Toby told April if she'd just be still and listen, it would all become clear, and he went on. "See, these people probably aren't really my grandparents. But the thing is, they just found out that I—" There was a long pause, a long, suspicious pause, April thought, long enough for Toby to cook up the next part of the story. "—that I have royal blood. Like, maybe I could be the next king of the Gypsies when I get to be eighteen years old."

"King of the Gypsies. Wow!" Elizabeth said.

April didn't say anything, but what she thought of saying was, "Sure you could. And how about an alien from outer space, while you're at it?" Ken and Melanie didn't say anything, but April could tell that they weren't exactly buying Toby's story either.

"But why'd these guys want to kidnap you?" Ken asked.

Toby looked at Ken as though he couldn't believe his best friend was asking such a dumb question. "So they could be—like, the power behind the throne. You know, like being the Royal Grandparents. That sort of thing. Anyway, what they did was threaten my father because he said he wouldn't let me go with them."

"Threaten?" Melanie asked.

"Yeah." Toby drew a finger across his throat and made a gruesome gurgling noise. "They're really desperate people, I guess."

Ken looked puzzled and worried. "But all you told me was that your grandparents had shown up, and you didn't want anybody else to know about them because they were so boring."

"Right. That's all I knew about them at first. The boring part. But then, when I found out what they were really up to, I knew I had to get out of there. So I packed up some stuff, and when it was almost morning, I split. I spent last night under the bridge down by the railroad track, but there were some other guys there." Toby's eyes dropped, but before they did, for just a second, Melanie thought she saw something strange in them. Something like terror. "Some pretty weird characters sleep under that bridge. So then this morning I came here." He grinned. "And since then I've been sharing Bear's blankets and mattress." He scratched again and grinned. "Not to mention his fleas."

"But what are you going to do now?" Ken asked. "They'll probably look for you here. I mean the police will, at least." He paused. "You could come home with me," he said. "My mom would probably—"

"No," Toby said quickly. "No. She'd tell. And besides, I wouldn't want to put you guys in danger too. These so-called grandparents of mine have some hit men who are real scary types."

"Hit men?" Elizabeth looked puzzled.

"Yeah, you know. Bump-off artists? Hired guns?"

Elizabeth still didn't get it.

"Liquidators? Terminators? Murderers? Get it?"

Elizabeth got it. "Murderers?" she breathed.

"How do you know?" April asked. "I mean, how do you know your grandparents have hit men?"

"Because I saw them. They brought them along when they came to our place. There were two of them. They were, you know, real bloodthirsty types." Toby shuddered as if he was remembering something horrible. "So that's why I can't go home with any of you. And you can't tell

90

anyone about seeing me. Okay? Not even my dad. Especially not my dad."

Somehow, against her will, April found herself almost believing Toby's ridiculous story. Or at least parts of it. The part you almost had to believe was that Toby was really worried or scared about something. Checking Melanie's face, April thought she could tell that Melanie was believing that part, too.

Suddenly Melanie looked at her watch and caught her breath. "We have to go," she said. "My folks will be out looking for us. Hey, where's Marshall?"

They found him behind the mural, sound asleep on Bear's bed. He was still only half awake when they walked him across the yard. They were all going out the gate when Ken suddenly turned back. "Will you be all right, Tobe? I mean it's supposed to get pretty cold tonight."

"I'll be great," Toby said. "I've got all those old blankets—and Bear. Bear's better than an electric blanket. There is one thing, though. If any of you could come back here later on and bring me something to eat, it sure would be great. Just—a piece of bread, or anything." Toby grinned and shrugged, trying to make a joke of it, but you could tell by the way he swallowed that just thinking about eating a piece of bread was making him drool.

They all said they'd help. Ken said he'd be back with food for sure, and April and Melanie said they thought they could gather up some stuff and sneak out long enough to bring it over. Elizabeth said she probably couldn't come, but their refrigerator was full of leftovers from the big family banquet in San Francisco, and she could put a bag of stuff out in the hall for April and Melanie to pick up.

"Hey, I can't wait," Toby said. Then he grinned and added, "I was getting pretty tired of dog kibble."

Melanie gave April a look that said she didn't know whether to laugh or cry. April knew what she meant. Not that she was about to cry over the mess old Alvillar had gotten himself into, but at the same time the thought of anybody being out alone on the streets at night, cold and hungry and frightened. . . . She shivered.

On the way home April and Melanie made careful plans, and when they arrived at the door of the Rosses' apartment, they went over their strategy once more. Exactly what they would say to the grown-ups, and when and how they would meet. Then, as Melanie unlocked the door, April gave Marshall, who was still practically sleepwalking, a small shake.

"Remember?" she said. "Don't tell anybody about Toby."

Marshall's drooping eyelids lifted slightly. "I remember," he mumbled. "If I tell, they'll take him to the pound."

Melanie rolled her eyes at April, pushed Marshall through the door, and closed it behind him. "About what Toby said—you know, about why he ran away. . . . Do you believe him?"

"Believe him?" April sniffed. "All that royalty stuff? Are you kidding?" She paused, frowning. "But there was a part of it—the part about him being really scared."

"Yes. That's what I think. What I think is—"

"Melanie." It was Melanie's mom's voice. "Melanie, are you out there?"

Melanie went in, waving a silent good-bye over her shoulder.

At dinner that night while April was trying to concentrate on what parts of her dinner she might be able to save for Toby, Caroline kept asking questions about who had been in the office when she'd been called in and what they'd asked about. And she also asked quite a few questions about Toby's father.

"You know Toby and you've met Mr. Alvillar," Caroline said. "What do you think? Some people I've talked to seem to think that he isn't much of a father and that he might be to blame for Toby's disappearance, in one way or another."

April shook her head and then caught herself just in time to keep from saying, "That's not what Toby says." Caught herself, and stuffed her mouth so full she wouldn't be able to say anything until she'd had more time to think about a safe answer. After she'd chewed slowly and carefully for several seconds, she said, "Well, I have heard Toby complaining about his dad, but mostly just stuff like his cooking. I've heard Toby say his dad is really a lousy cook."

After Caroline agreed that his dad's cooking probably wasn't the reason Toby disappeared, April finally managed to change the subject.

Fourteen

AFTER DINNER THAT night Melanie managed to stuff some bread, a big hunk of cheese, and a couple of apples into a paper bag and hide it under her jacket on the bench of the hall tree. Then, following their plan, at exactly seven-thirty she got permission to go up to April's for a few minutes, at the very same time April was getting permission to run down to her place. It worked perfectly. Just as Melanie stuck her head out the door, she began to hear quiet footsteps coming down from the third floor, and seconds later they arrived together in the lobby.

"Hey, great," she whispered. "I've got bread and cheese and apples. What do you have?"

"Not too much," April said. "Just two humongous doughnuts and a can of Pepsi. Oh yeah, and my carrot sticks from dinner. Come on. Let's see what Elizabeth dug up."

In the downstairs hall they found a large bag under Elizabeth's little sister's tricycle, just where she'd said it would be. Good old Elizabeth. Then they were off and running.

It was scary running down the alley. At first there was a little light from the streetlamps on Orchard Avenue, but after a few yards the light grew dimmer and the shadows longer and blacker. It was the first time April had been in the alley after dark since—but she wasn't going to think about that. Within a very few minutes they were knocking softly on the gate of the Gypsy Camp. Almost immediately it opened a crack and a flashlight beam shone on their faces.

"Quick!" Toby's fiery Gypsy eyes gleamed in the dim light like the eyes of a wild animal. A starving wild animal. "Come on in," he whispered hungrily as he grabbed the bags and led the way to the shed with Bear bouncing enthusiastically around all three of them. "Here, hold this," Toby said, handing his flashlight to Melanie. Then he sat down, put everything on his lap, and began to open the bags one at a time, grinning and chuckling and making comments like, "Hey, a doughnut. Awesome! Wow, cheese. Fantastic. Chinese, my favorite," and "Get out of there, Bear. That isn't for you." Grabbing one of the doughnuts, he took a big bite and then sprayed doughnut crumbs in every direction as he said, "Hey, sit down and dig in. Looks like there's plenty here for everybody."

"Oh, we can't," Melanie said. "We have to get right back. Nobody knows we're here."

April agreed. "If we're not back in five minutes, we're all in deep trouble. Come on, Melanie. Let's get going. So long."

Toby waved briefly, muttered a few doughnut-muffled syllables, and went back to serious eating.

At the gate April and Melanie stopped long enough to peer in both directions before they eased out cautiously and took off into a dim, shadow-haunted world. Running as fast as they dared in the murky light, they sped down the driveway with fear nipping at their heels, turned out into the alley, and picked up speed until suddenly they slid to a stop. Clutching each other, they crouched in terror, straining their ears to hear, over their own thundering hearts and rasping breath, the sound of—footsteps. Yes, footsteps, faint at first but definitely coming in their direction. The sound of running feet getting louder and louder, and nearer and nearer until something careened around the corner, loomed shapelessly in the near darkness, and almost ran right over them. It was Ken, of course.

When he rounded the corner, Ken was almost running blind, his line of vision partly obscured by the huge bag he was carrying. A plastic bag that looked big enough to carry rations for a Boy Scout wilderness weekend. "*Sheesh!*" he said, sliding to a stop. "Where'd you guys come from? I almost ran into you." He looked them over. "You going or coming?"

"Going," April managed in a squeaky voice. "We've already been there."

Lowering his voice, Ken asked, "How's Toby? Is he starving?"

"Not anymore," Melanie said. "Come on, April. We've got to go. Now!"

They ran again then, around the corner, down the dark alley, out onto Orchard Avenue, up the steps, and safely back into the lobby of the Casa Rosada.

"Whew," Melanie said, taking off her jacket. "I hope we don't have to do that anymore."

April knew what she meant. The alley after dark was scary enough no matter what you were doing, but somehow running made it even more terrifying. "After this, we're going to have to figure out a way to feed Toby before dark."

As Melanie opened her front door, she said, "I know. Let's have a Feeding Toby Conference tomorrow. Right after school, on the playground, before everybody splits for home. We can decide who'll feed him and when and stuff like that. Okay?"

"Okay, right after school," April agreed, but a minute later as she was climbing up to the third floor, it occurred to her that getting Kamata to attend an otherwise all-girl playground conference was not going to be all that easy. Actually, not going to be *possible,* would be more like it.

"Ken won't come to the conference," she told Melanie and Elizabeth the next morning on the way to school. "You know that, don't you? Do you really think the great he-man, macho, all-star athlete is going to stand around on the playground whispering to three girls right out there in front of everybody? Come on, gimme a break! It'll never happen. The three of us will just have to decide what to do and then send Kamata a note, or something."

On second thought, Melanie had to agree. "I guess you're probably right," she said. "He'll never do it." But only a minute or two later, when they happened to see Ken parking his bike in the school's bike rack, she changed her mind. "We ought to tell him about it, though. That we're going to have a Toby conference, I mean."

April bowed and gestured. "Okay. Go on, be my guest. You tell him."

"Okay, I will," Melanie said stubbornly. As she ran off toward the bike rack, April told herself smugly that she, April Hall, had too much sense to risk being snubbed or insulted right out there in front of the school and everybody. Instead, she would just wait right here and watch

Melanie make a fool of herself. So she sat down on the bus bench, pulled Elizabeth down beside her, and waited. A minute or two later Melanie came back looking not so much insulted and angry as scared.

"What is it?" April asked.

Melanie's high-flying eyebrows were tucked into a worried frown. "He said—he said he'd be there." She shook her head unbelievingly. "At the conference. I mean, Ken must be worried to death."

"Yeah." April felt something like a cold, clammy finger of doom trace its way up her backbone. "I know what you mean."

As soon as school was out that day, April and Melanie met Elizabeth outside the fourth-grade room and headed for a special spot just below the windows on the south side of the building. Being a little too close to the principal's office for comfort, it had never been a popular hangout spot, which tended to make it a little more private. Right after classes let out, most of the schoolyard was crowded with kids who had signed up for after-school activities, but just as April and Melanie had hoped, their chosen area was still fairly deserted. But the bad news was there was no sign of Ken.

Several minutes went by and still no Ken. Groups of fifth- and sixth-grade girls straggled out to join after-school tether ball, and a bunch of boys headed for the basketball courts. The girls were about to give up when suddenly Ken burst into view, running at top speed. Halfway across the yard he changed course slightly and swerved in their direction.

"Look," he said almost before he'd stopped running,

"we've got to get Toby out of there, right away. We've got to think of someplace else for him to go." Drowning out a chorus of "Why?" and "Where can he go?" he rushed on, "I was going past the office just now and Mr. Adams nabbed me again. And two guys were in there with him. And this time I'm sure they really were police detectives. I think somebody must have ratted about—you know where. We've got to get him out of there, as fast as we can." Then, without even answering one question, he went on running, this time headed for the schoolyard exit and the bicycle rack.

After a frozen moment April said, "Come on. Let's go. Hurry!" And they did. Since it was Mr. Ross's day to take care of Marshall, they didn't have to stop at the day-care center, but even with almost nonstop running they didn't beat Ken on his bicycle. When, breathless and exhausted, they turned into the Professor's driveway, Ken was already there. But he wasn't the only one.

A dusty gray car was parked halfway down the Professor's driveway, and two strange men in sinister-looking business suits were standing beside it. One of the men was holding the handlebars of Ken's bicycle as if to keep him from escaping. Ken was talking, that much was obvious. But just how much he was saying, how much he was giving away, it was impossible to tell.

April grabbed Elizabeth and Melanie and tried to pull them back out of sight, but it was too late. They'd been seen.

"Girls!" one of the men shouted. "Come here! We need to talk to you."

April's mind said "run," but her body decided against it.

She was too tired to run another step. Slowly and reluctantly, the three girls moved forward.

"Policemen?" Melanie gasped breathlessly, and April nodded.

"Probably," she whispered back, trying not to listen to the crazy voice in the back of her mind that added, "or hit men."

Fifteen

THE TWO MEN were both dressed in scruffy, colorless suits, but in other ways they were very different. One was short and bald with a bulldog scowl and a lopsided nose. The other was tall and bony with eyes and lips that kept twitching, as if he were about to start laughing. As if he thought scaring a bunch of kids to death was lots of fun.

"Well, well," the crooked-nosed one said. "You girls are a bit out of breath. What was the big hurry?"

Out of breath. That was it. Pretending she was too breathless to talk, April clutched her throat and shook her head, and Melanie and Elizabeth did the same thing. It didn't take much acting. Running all that way, then the shock of seeing poor old Ken in the clutches of two strange men. . . . April gasped and staggered, as if she were about to pass out.

"Okay, take five," the tall man said. "Catch your breath." But then, long before five minutes had passed, he went on, "All right. Ready to talk now? We understand you kids know something about this fenced area. Just tell us how we get in here. Apparently there's a locked dead bolt on the other side of the gate. Which would seem to mean there's someone in there, wouldn't it? So, who is it?" He looked at Melanie.

Melanie shook her head. "I don't know," she whispered.

The men looked at Ken. "Nobody," he said defiantly. "Nobody's in there."

And then it was April's turn, and with sudden inspiration she said, "Our dog. That's where we keep our dog."

The other man, the one with the bald head and the bashed-in nose, gave a sneering laugh. "And I suppose this superintelligent dog closes the dead bolt behind you after you go out?"

"Uh, not exactly. But sometimes he just jiggles the door"—she pawed the air, imitating a dog pawing on a door—"and I guess it sort of locks itself."

"Is that right?" The tall man was obviously amused again. The short one with the beat-up nose smirked.

"Oh, is that so?" he said. "Here, Mac, give me a leg up. Think I'll try a little bolt jiggling myself." Stepping in his partner's linked hands, he grabbed the top of the gate and pulled himself up until he could reach over and open the dead bolt. After he'd dropped back down, he grinned and rubbed his hands together like a cartoon villain who just can't wait to do something mean and nasty. "Okay," he said with more hand rubbing. "Let's just see this talented dog of yours." He swaggered to the gate, pushed it open, stepped inside, and a split second later jumped back out, slamming the gate behind him.

"There *is* a dog in there," he admitted, smiling sheepishly. "A big one."

The tall man grinned as if something was really funny. Maybe as if he knew that Crooked Nose had some kind of a special problem where dogs were concerned. "Here, let me," he said, and pushed the gate open.

Of course Bear greeted him with his usual friendly enthusiasm, jumping around and wagging his stub of a tail. As he bounced happily around the two men, Melanie gave April a disgusted look that said something like, "Some watchdog." April nodded. Bear would probably do the same thing if Frankenstein's monster dropped in for a visit.

But if Bear wasn't very good at recognizing an enemy, he did seem to be able to tune in on how his friends were feeling. As soon as the four kids entered the yard, he seemed to sense that something was wrong. Pausing suddenly in midprance, he sniffed mournfully at each of them, tucked his tail, and crept off to disappear behind the Gypsy caravan mural.

Behind the mural, where Toby must be too! Where Toby had to be! There was absolutely nothing else in the shed or yard big enough to hide something the size of a kid. April hoped she hadn't been staring at the caravan, but maybe she had been, because suddenly Crooked Nose was, too.

"What's with the work of art?" he said, pointing at the mural.

"It's a picture of a Gypsy caravan." April gulped. Her heart was still pounding, but her breath was a little more under control now. "It's—it's for a project on Gypsies we're doing." The hit men looked faintly interested, particularly the tall one.

"A project?" he asked.

"Yes," April went on desperately, "a school project. We've been getting it ready out here in the shed because we don't want anybody to see it until—until . . ." She was running out of ideas—looking around frantically at the other kids, asking them to help. To come to her rescue and think up more things to keep the policemen or hired guns or whatever talking instead of looking around. Instead of looking behind the mural, where a terror-stricken Toby must be crouching on Bear's bed, waiting to be caught. Nobody picked up the ball, so she struggled on. "See, there's going to be this big contest to see who can make the best . . ." But Crooked Nose had stopped listening and was moving toward the shed. "The best project," April limped on. Crooked Nose walked to the back of the shed and looked behind the mural. Looked—stared—and then came back to where his partner was waiting.

"Nobody there," he said. "Except for the dog."

The two men turned to look from one kid to the other. Long, hard, accusing looks.

Ken made a swallowing noise before he said, "Yeah. That's what we've been trying to tell you. Nobody—except for the dog."

Silence. For a long moment no one said anything while the two men checked out the storage yard again. The almost-empty yard with its tall, sturdy board fence topped by two strands of barbed wire. Then the tall guy said, "Okay, kids. The Alvillar boy isn't here—at the moment. But I think we all know that you kids know a lot more about his disappearance than you're saying. And if you do, you'd better come clean. For your own sakes as well as for Alvillar's." He looked at all their faces, one at a time, and stopped at—tiny little fourth-grade Elizabeth. Going over to her, he bent down to her level, and making his voice soft and gentle, he said, "You look like a nice little girl. Not the kind of kid who would want a friend of yours to be in a lot of danger. And a lot of danger is just what Tobias Alvillar is going to be in if he doesn't give himself up and get back home where he belongs. So why don't you just tell me . . ."

Elizabeth began to cry. "I don't know where he is." She sobbed wildly. "I don't know how . . ."

"Leave her alone!" Melanie didn't get angry often, but when she did, look out! Pushing in front of the tall man, she put her arms around Elizabeth and pulled her away. Then while Elizabeth sobbed on her shoulder, she turned back to glare fiercely at both of the men. "Now look what you've done," she said. "You—you big goons!"

The two men stared at Melanie, whispered together for a minute or two, and headed for the gate. Just before they went out the tall one stopped long enough to say, "Okay. Okay. But if you kids—if any one of you kids—change your mind about talking, just call this number." Taking a card out of his pocket, he came back and shoved it into the pocket of Ken's jacket. Then he went on out and closed the gate behind him.

Inside the Gypsy Camp no one said anything until they heard a car motor starting up and then the fading sound of tires on gravel. Ken whacked Melanie on the back.

"Hey, you were great," he said. "You really cooled those bums."

"Who were those guys, anyway?" April asked.

"They're the detectives I told you about. You know, the ones who were in the principal's office. The ones who asked me about a kids' hangout behind a store on Orchard Avenue. Like somebody had ratted or something." He looked around accusingly, but everyone quickly shook their heads. "That's why I told you we had to get Toby out before they showed up here."

"How do you know they're really police detectives?" April asked suspiciously.

"Well, that's what Mr. Adams said they were. And they had badges. At least the tall one did. When they first drove up, he showed it to me."

"*Hummph.*" April made a noise that meant "If you want to believe that." Out loud she said, "It's easy to get a phony badge. I got one once in a box of cereal. So, how do we know they weren't really hit men, like Toby said?"

Ken reached into his pocket and pulled out the tall guy's card. "See, it says right here, 'Detective James Arnold. Precinct 7.'"

April snatched the card, read it, and handed it back. "Well, okay, if you want to believe everything you read. I'll bet a lot of people carry phony ID cards. You don't really think hit men go around handing out real business cards, do you? You know, like 'Enemies bumped off. While you wait.'"

Melanie was still patting Elizabeth's back and whispering in her ear. Elizabeth's sobs had quieted, and now she caught her breath, gulped, and said, "Maybe what that man said is true. Maybe Toby is in danger." Wiping her eyes, she looked around the yard. "Where is he?" She looked at Ken. "Where did he go?"

Ken looked around, too. Then he ran to the back of the shed and disappeared behind the mural. A second later he came out shaking his head.

"Good move, Kamata," April said sarcastically. "I mean,

just in case that guy overlooked him or something? Like, he might have been hiding under a blanket or behind the dog dish?"

Ken gave her a blank stare. "Yeah," he said. "Or he might have left a clue. Like a note or at least some of his stuff. Like his flashlight or backpack. But he didn't. All his stuff is gone, except for a couple of torn-up bags."

They all went to look then, but Ken was right. Except for the bags, there was no sign of Toby's ever having been there.

"That probably means he must have left earlier," Melanie said. "Before any of us got here, because he wouldn't have had time to gather everything up if he had to leave in a hurry."

Ken stared at her for a moment before he slowly shook his head. "No. I don't think so. When I first got here, the dead bolt was locked, so I knocked on the gate, and I'm sure, well, almost sure, I heard Toby say, 'Who is it?' And I said, 'It's Ken.' But just then those guys drove up, and after that I didn't hear anything more."

"Maybe what you heard was Bear," April said. Every one glared at her as if they thought she was trying to make a joke when it was obviously no time to be funny. "No," she explained impatiently, "I didn't mean Bear said, 'Who is it?' I just meant maybe he made a whining noise that sounded like someone talking. Dogs can do that some-times."

Ken was still shaking his head. "No. It didn't sound like that. I guess I must have imagined it. I think Toby must have split a long time ago. Like while we were still at school, maybe."

They were all agreeing, until suddenly a small weepy voice said, "But what about the bolt?"

They all turned to stare at Elizabeth and then at the dead bolt, which had definitely been closed when the two men arrived only a few minutes before.

"How . . . ?" someone said, and they all nodded.

"Hey," April said, "I'll bet he went out earlier through the gate, and then he got a box or something to stand on and reached back over the top to shut it. Like that other guy did."

"No. No way," Ken said. "It would have to have been a really humongous box for him to reach that far. I mean, too big for him to carry all by himself."

So that was out. Melanie suggested a ladder, but no one could think of a place where Toby might have found a ladder without being seen by someone who would probably have recognized him. And besides, why would he want to do that? Why would he want to go out and then go to all the trouble to leave the gate locked from the inside?

"But he could have climbed *out* over the gate and left it locked," Melanie suggested. "If he carried something over to the gate to climb up on, it would . . ." She stopped to stare at the objects in the shed that might have served that purpose, the birdbath and the old box that had been Set's altar, and April finished the sentence for her, ". . . it would still be sitting there by the gate."

Melanie sighed and said, "Well, I guess it's just another mystery." Which was exactly what April was thinking too. Just one more mystery to add to the main one about why Toby ran away in the first place. April was about to ask Ken and Elizabeth if they were thinking the same thing when

Bear barked, ran to the gate, and cocked his head as if he was listening.

And then they heard it too. Footsteps. Gravel-crunching footsteps coming down the driveway and approaching the gate.

"Oh no!" Elizabeth's voice quavered. "They're coming back."

"Or else maybe . . . ," April said, "maybe it's Toby?"

Ken was grinning eagerly. "Yeah, I'll bet it is." He raised his voice to a loud whisper. "Come on in, Alvillar. The gate's unlatched."

When the gate opened, it was Alvillar, all right. But it wasn't Toby.

Sixteen

WHEN KEN YELLED, "Come on in, Alvillar," the guy who walked into the Gypsy Camp was a full-grown man. The weird-looking, bushy-haired full-grown man who happened to be Toby's father. Closing the gate behind him, Andre Alvillar ignored Bear's bouncing greeting and looked around the yard. His Toby-like eyes, dark but speckled with flecks of light, moved quickly from place to place and person to person.

Watching the strange eyes shadowed by masses of hair and beard, April began to be aware of rumors drifting through her mind. Scary, stealthy thoughts, flitting here and there like the wings of tiny, vicious bats. Rumors about the kinds of things a person might do who looked and lived so differently from the way the parents of other kids did and who didn't seem to care at all what other people thought of him. When the dark eyes touched hers, she shivered, but they moved on, and when they stopped, they were on Ken.

" 'Come on in, Alvillar'?" he asked. "Isn't that what I heard you say, Ken?"

Ken nodded. "Yeah, but I meant . . . That is—I thought it might be Toby. I was hoping it would be, anyhow."

"Then you don't know where he is?"

Ken shook his head, and one by one the others did, too, as the fiery eyes moved from face to face.

It wasn't a lie. They didn't know. Not at the moment. And if they really didn't know where Toby was right now, it surely wasn't a lie not to mention that they had known just last night. But then, as if he were reading their minds, Andre Alvillar said, "But you *have* seen him. Since the thirty-first, that is? Since the night he disappeared?"

Toby had said not to tell anyone they'd seen him, *especially* his father, so no one said yes, but no one said no, either. Instead, they all looked at one another—hoping to let someone else decide how to deal with the question. At least that was what April was doing, and she was sure the others were, too. But as it turned out, they didn't have to answer because Andre Alvillar seemed to have read their minds. Or perhaps their faces.

"You have," he said, nodding slowly. "Yes, *yes!* I see that you have."

April had been bracing herself for him to yell at them for not letting him know, or even to grill them about where and when they'd last seen Toby. But, instead, he did a very weird thing. Turning away, he walked across the yard, pounding his right fist into his open left hand. His face was turned away, but what he was doing looked like anger. When he turned, April caught a glimpse of white teeth, as if, behind all that curly black hair, he was almost smiling. Or maybe growling? A shiver crawled up April's back, and when she glanced at Melanie, she guessed that Melanie was feeling the same kind of thing.

When he was almost to the fence, Alvillar turned and came back, and then, as he reached the center of the yard, he did another strange thing. Putting his hand to his forehead, he took a deep breath and sat down on the ground. Just sat flat down without saying anything, and went on sitting there staring into space, as if sitting flat down on the dusty ground were a perfectly normal thing for a grown person to do.

So Andre Alvillar sat on the ground staring at nothing, and the four kids stared at him, and after what seemed like an incredibly long time, he took another deep breath, sighed, and said, "Well, at least he wasn't kidnapped. We do know that?"

For several long seconds no one said anything. For just a moment April thought of saying, "Well, we did last night, anyway," before she realized what a lot of other questions that would bring up. Congratulating herself on remembering to keep her mouth shut, she only clenched her teeth and shrugged. But this time Melanie seemed to have forgotten.

"Did *you* think he might be kidnapped?" Melanie asked.

The lean, bony face, like Sherlock Holmes's, only a lot hairier, turned toward Melanie. "Yes," he said. "I did think it was a possibility."

"Why?" This time Ken was asking a question.

Alvillar thought for a moment before he said, "It's rather complicated, Ken. I'm not sure I can go into it right now, but it has to do with his grandparents. With Toby's maternal grandparents. They've been trying to get legal custody of Toby."

April and Melanie exchanged amazed glances. Glances that said how surprised they were that Toby had been telling the truth, or at least a lot more of the truth than anyone had believed.

"Legal custody?" Elizabeth whispered to Melanie.

But it was Andre Alvillar who answered. "Adoption," he said. "They wanted me to give up my right to Toby as my son, to make it possible for them to adopt him legally. But I refused, of course."

"But Toby didn't want to be adopted," Ken said. It was a statement but also a kind of question.

Alvillar shook his head. "No. No, indeed. He made that quite clear." A brief facial movement twitched the bushy beard. "As a matter of fact he told me that if he had to live with his grandparents, he'd run away and join the Gypsies." He gestured toward the mural. "That's why I thought of coming here to this—" He paused, looking around the yard. "To this Gypsy community. But obviously he isn't here."

Everyone nodded.

"At least not at the moment."

The nods were less confident.

"But he has been here?"

No nods, but no firm shakes either. Andre Alvillar stared at their faces for a long time before he sighed and got to his feet. "I think I understand," he said. "And it's obvious that I've created an ethical dilemma, so we'll leave it at that for now." He looked around again, holding their eyes with his strange magnetic stare. "However, I'm glad to know that he has been seen quite recently, alive and well?" It sounded like a question. A question that no one answered except for some confused head twitches, half nod and half shake. "But

113

if you should see Toby again in the near future, will you please ask him to let me know that he is alive and well?" Suddenly stepping closer, Andre Alvillar grabbed Ken's shoulder with one hand and April's arm with the other. "You must promise me that much, Ken!" His burning eyes moved to April. "And you too. You must promise!"

April found herself nodding helplessly, and then the gate creaked open and the weird bushy-haired man was gone.

Ken was the first one to say anything. What he said was, "*Sheesh*! Ethical di—something or other. What does that mean?"

Nobody knew. "I'll look it up," Melanie said. "As soon as we get home. Eth-i-cal di-lem-ma. Help me remember, April."

April said she would. But at the moment what she really wanted to know was just how much of the stuff Toby had told them was true. "Like, all that crazy stuff about his grandparents wanting to get him so they could be the power behind the throne." She threw up her hands. "Nobody believed that for a minute. Right? And now it looks like maybe it's the truth, or at least part of it is. So what about the rest? About him being the next king of the Gypsies, or whatever."

"Naw." Ken shook his head. "That's not the truth. I mean, if Tobe had known that he was going to be a king someday, he'd have told me a long time ago. Tobe and I always tell each other important stuff like that."

"But maybe he just found out about being king," Melanie said. "Didn't he say his grandparents just found out about it? That kind of makes sense. Because if people had known about it all along, why didn't his grandparents try to get him a long time ago?" Everyone agreed that *did* make sense. Melanie was good at logical stuff like that.

"So maybe he really did run away because he didn't want to go live with—" Elizabeth started before Melanie interrupted her.

"But that can't be it," Melanie said. "His dad said he refused to let them have him. They couldn't *make* Toby go live with them if his father wouldn't give his permission, could they?"

Lots of head shakes. "There just isn't any sensible explanation," April said. "Like I said, it's just all a big mystery."

"No." Ken was frowning. Ken didn't like mysteries any more than he liked ancient ceremonies and other off-the-wall kooky stuff. "No, not all of it," he said. "We know some things for sure. Like that Toby wasn't really kidnapped. That's one thing we know for sure. And . . ."

"And that's about it," April said. "We don't know if he really ran away to keep from being kidnapped, like he said. And we don't know how much of what he told us was a lie." She thought for a moment. "And I guess we don't really know if his father was lying about not letting him be adopted." She rolled her eyes knowingly. "Maybe his father *was* lying and what he was really planning to do was to sell him off to his rich relatives, like he was a used car or something."

It was a new idea, and a shocking one. They were still considering the possibility when suddenly Elizabeth said, "Look. Look at Bear."

They all looked. On the other side of the storage yard Bear was scratching the fence with both front feet. At the foot of the fence just below the plank that had once been the only entrance to the Land of Egypt. Everyone gasped and ran.

A moment later they were all clustered around the plank which, before the fence had been repaired, had been loose at the bottom so that it could be swung to one side. A board that once again seemed to be a little bit loose. Sure enough, when Ken gave it a good whack with his closed fist, it came loose with a rusty creak and swung back, leaving a very familiar narrow entryway.

"So that's it," Melanie whispered. "That's how he got out. Maybe he *was* in here when Ken knocked, and he did say, 'Who is it?' and then he heard those detective guys talking and he just squeezed out through here."

"Yeah," Ken said. "You know what I bet? I bet he knocked this board loose again way ahead of time. Like yesterday or something. You know, got it ready, just in case. Just in case he ever needed an escape route. Tobe's the kind of guy who would think of doing something like that. So then, when he heard those dudes talking to me, he grabbed his stuff and slipped out and ran."

They all agreed that was probably it. "But where do you suppose he went?" April asked. Pushing the board aside, she slipped out into the empty, deserted alley. One at a time, the others followed her, sliding through easily except for Ken, who had always been a little too broad for such a narrow opening. While he was squeezing his way through, Bear tried to follow, but they shoved him back inside and put the plank back over the opening.

"He can't have gotten very far," Ken said. "We could search up and down the alley anyway."

116

April didn't agree. "Not very far?" she said. "Toby's a fast runner. He could be miles from here by now."

Elizabeth nodded. "Anyway, I can't help search right now. I have to get home right away. I promised my mom I'd come straight home. She's been real nervous about kidnappers lately."

"Me too," Melanie said. "I have to get going. But maybe tomorrow after school we could come back and do a big search. I think my folks would let me come back to the Gypsy Camp tomorrow if we promise to all stay together."

"Okay," Ken said. "But I'm going to look around a little. Like, maybe he's not far from here, hiding behind some garbage cans or something."

So Ken went off down the alley, and the three girls ran toward the Casa Rosada while, behind the fence, Bear sat near the loose plank and whined softly to himself.

Seventeen

THAT AFTERNOON, at the very moment when Ken was arriving at the gate of the Gypsy Camp, Toby had been rearranging the stuff in his backpack, getting it ready in case he had to make a quick exit. Actually there wasn't much to arrange. On New Year's Eve, when he finally realized that the only thing he could do was run away, it was already so late that he barely had time to throw a comb, a few socks, an extra pair of jeans, and a flashlight into his pack. Not much to start your whole life over with. But there it was, all his worldly goods, taking up no more than a couple of inches at the bottom of the beat-up old backpack.

But now, of course, thanks to the rest of the Gypsies, there was also quite a bit of food. He peered into each of the bags, three paper ones and Ken's king-sized plastic job. The egg rolls were all gone and the doughnuts, but there were still a few cookies, two apples, a good-sized piece of cheese, and a big chunk of French bread. It would all fit into one of the paper bags now, so he consolidated, tearing open the others to let Bear get at the crumbs. Then he finished the job by zipping up the pockets and adjusting the straps. Everything was ready if he had to make a fast getaway. And just barely in time.

He heard the bicycle first, a whir of gears and then the

118

squeal of brakes and skid of tires on gravel. It definitely sounded like Ken, particularly the squeal and skid. Ken was that kind of a bike jockey. He'd just called, "Who is it?" and was on his way to the gate when suddenly the other noises began to kick in. The sound of a motor first, the crunch of wheels on gravel, the slamming of car doors, and then the voices. Strange men's voices!

He waited long enough to be sure, until he heard one of them mention his name, actually say something about Tobias Alvillar, before he grabbed his backpack and ran for it. Ran right to the old entrance he'd had the good sense to put back into working order earlier that same day, just in case something like this should happen.

Of course Bear tried to come with him, but he pushed him back and slid the plank into place. A split second later he was off around the corner and out into the main alley, running in a kind of terror-stricken panic like a poor hunted fox. But he hadn't gone far before he spotted a kind of fox hole. Actually, a long section of cement drainage pipe lying along the edge of the alley waiting for the new sewer system to go in. After throwing his backpack as far back into the pipe as he could, he wiggled and squirmed his way in after it.

He stayed in the pipe for quite a long time. It was a fairly tight fit, big for a pipe, but not all that big. Which was a good thing actually, since it might not even be considered worth investigating as a possible hiding place. At least not by the guys whose voices he'd heard—big, deep voices that probably came from big, deep chests. Guys who might have forgotten how small a space a skinny kid could squeeze himself into if he was desperate enough. As a matter of fact the kind of space, it occurred to him a few minutes later, that even a skinny kid might have a little bit of trouble getting back out of.

He wondered about that for a while—the getting-out problem—before he got up his nerve to give it a try. But then, just as he started to claw and wiggle backward down the pipe, he began to hear footsteps. The footsteps went past him down the alley and then slowly came back, as if the person was looking for something. With fear suddenly tightening his throat, he frantically clawed and wiggled back the other way and then lay still, holding his breath and straining his ears. But after the footsteps faded away for the second time and didn't come back, his panic slowly began to fade.

Some time later Toby began to feel hungry and made the discovery that unzipping a backpack and getting out a paper sack full of food while lying flat on your face was surprisingly difficult. And eating wasn't all that easy either. But he went on eating, for lack of anything better to do, until it occurred to him that it might not be the best place in the world to put on a lot of weight. So he pushed what was left, actually nothing but a big chunk of French bread, back into the pack and went on lying there, waiting and listening and, after a long while, even getting a little sleepy. Not that he was going to go to sleep. No chance. Not a chance in the world that a poor fugitive trapped in a sewer pipe could actually fall asleep. . . .

Some time later he woke up feeling as though quite a bit of time had passed. Actually, it seemed like forever. He was cold and stiff and . . . And just beyond his feet there was this weird snuffling and clawing noise as if some kind of wild animal were trying to crawl into the pipe with him. He was desperately trying to pull his feet up out of reach when the whimpering started. It was a very familiar whimper.

"Bear, you klutz," he whispered. "How'd you get out?" But actually he had a pretty good idea. Leaving in such a hurry, he probably hadn't replaced the plank carefully enough, and the big mutt had pushed it open and escaped.

Just as he'd feared, wiggling his way backward out of the pipe wasn't a piece of cake, particularly not with Bear bouncing around on the parts of him that were already out. But then a surprising thing happened. When Toby's head finally emerged from the pipe, Bear only waited long enough to give him a big sloppy greeting all over both cheeks before he pulled away and started off up the alley at a steady trot.

"Come back here," Toby called softly, but Bear didn't come. He'd heard all right, that was for sure, because he stopped and looked back. But then he only whined coaxingly and set off again, moving away into the deepening shadows of evening. Toby hurriedly finished fishing his backpack out of the pipe, shrugged himself into it, and after glancing up and down the dimly lit, deserted alley, ran after the rapidly disappearing dog.

What happened in the next half hour was entirely Bear's fault. Trotting along just a few yards ahead and coming partway back whenever he got too far away, Old Shaggy Butt kept just out of reach. At first Toby followed because Bear was basically Marshall's dog, and he, Toby, didn't want to be responsible for letting him run away. His plan, if he had any, was just to catch up with the mutt and take him back home, before he even started deciding where to go or what to do himself. Running along after the sneaky animal, who somehow managed to keep a few feet ahead, he went up the alley, crossed over a parking lot, and came out on Norwich Avenue.

On Norwich, Toby's tactics had to change a little. For one thing, there were other people to deal with here. Hurrying people for the most part, on their way home for dinner probably, and not particularly interested in a boy and a dog. Not unless the boy was making himself conspicuous by sneaking up every time the dog stopped at a tree or fire hydrant and pouncing triumphantly, only to be faked out at the last moment. After trying it once or twice, and noticing that other pedestrians were stopping to enjoy the show, he decided to cool it. Bear, the old four-legged showboat, seemed to be getting a kick out of all the snickers and giggles, and Toby had to admit that he probably would have too, under normal circumstances. But at the moment, what with being a fugitive and all, attracting a lot of extra attention didn't seem like a totally great idea.

So then Toby just gave up trying to catch the dog. Slowing down to a nonchalant stroll, he tried to convince himself that if Bear ran off and left him, so much the better. He was tired of chasing the dumb flea trap. Let him run off and get lost, or get run over by a truck, or whatever. He, Toby Alvillar, couldn't care less.

But then, as soon as Toby began to slow down, Bear did, too. Acting as though he'd forgotten that Toby was anywhere around, he strolled down the sidewalk stopping to sniff and piddle at every tree trunk and lamppost. But always just out of grabbing range. At about that point, just thinking about how world-class stubborn Bear was being, Toby began to get angry. The frustrating mutt went along with you just fine as long as you were doing what he wanted you to, but if you started trying to call the shots, that was it. Forget it! *Finito!* Too bad for you, pal.

Muttering under his breath, stuff like, "Wait till I get my hands on you, you stupid hairball," Toby was still forcing himself to go on strolling when, about six blocks down Norwich, Bear suddenly crossed the avenue and turned up Arbor Street. Toby turned too, and it was right about then that he started to develop another reason to keep on following the stubborn dog. The thing was, stubborn or not, Bear did seem to know exactly where he was going. And under the circumstances, it was beginning to feel as if it was a good thing somebody did.

The first few blocks on Arbor went through a small business section, and because most of the shops had closed for the evening, there wasn't much pedestrian traffic. But Bear kept right on going toward the east where Arbor ran into the old industrial area on the edge of town. An unfamiliar area of mostly vacant lots and boarded-up warehouses with here and there a scattering of abandoned houses and small, crummy-looking stores.

By that time it was getting late. A clock in a liquor store window said almost eight. Eight o'clock on a very dark night. A thick bank of tule fog was oozing down from the north, and on Arbor, where the streetlamps were farther apart, it was definitely spooky. But, in a way, the fog was a good thing. If Toby couldn't see other people until he was practically on top of them, the good news was they couldn't see him either. A good thing, in case they happened to be the police out looking for a missing kid, or maybe somebody even more dangerous.

He wasn't exactly terrified the whole time, but now and then he wasn't far from it. Like when a patrol car cruised by and he had to duck behind a big debris box. Or another time when he was passing a crummy-type bar called the After Hours Club and a bunch of tough-looking guys stopped talking and stared at him as he walked by.

He probably would have gone back long before, but he knew Bear wouldn't come with him. Toby was just about to make up his mind to go back, even if he had to go alone, when Bear trotted eagerly off the sidewalk and onto a narrow path that led toward the rear of a small wooden building all by itself on an overgrown lot.

It wasn't a large building, hardly bigger than an ordinary house in fact, but it seemed to have a kind of tower over the front doors, and the windows were pointed at the top like the windows of churches. And there was a sign, too. By the faint glow of a distant streetlamp it was just possible to make out some faded lettering: Arbor Street Baptist. So it was, or had been, a church, but it wasn't likely that any services had been held there for a very long time. The paint was peeling from the walls, and heavy planks had been nailed across the doors and the bottom panes of the windows. Bear was closer now, only a few steps ahead, and recklessly Toby plunged after him. He almost had him once, but Bear pulled away and scooted on down the path that now was bordered by overgrown bushes, which shut out even the faint light of the distant streetlamps. A path that led into total darkness.

Toby was turning to go back, to get back to the light and

away from the threatening, enclosing underbrush, when suddenly something warm and furry pressed against his leg. Bear! He'd caught him at last. Grabbing the dog's collar with both hands, he was whispering, "Come on, Bear. Let's get out of here," when the big mutt lunged ahead so suddenly that Toby was pulled off-balance. He stumbled forward and found himself plunging down a short flight of stairs. Stumbling, lurching, and skidding, he lost his hold on Bear and crashed to a stop against a wall. And then, as he struggled to regain his balance, the wall turned out be a rough wooden door that jiggled and creaked and swung open onto black nothingness. Nothing except blinding darkness, a sense of deep, echoing space, and the smell of stale, damp air. He was backing away, feeling desperately for the first stair, when from somewhere in the dark, musty distance there came the sound of a match being struck, and then a strange, grating voice.

"Bruno," the voice creaked, "is that you? Where have you been, you ugly monster?"

Eighteen

IT WAS QUITE late that same night, at about the time that Toby was following Bear along Arbor Street, when the phone began ringing in the Halls' apartment on the third floor of the Casa Rosada apartment house. April's grandmother answered the ring and a moment later called, "April. Where are you? It's for you."

April had been out on the balcony at the time looking down on the shadow-haunted alley and thinking about Toby's being out there somewhere all alone in the dark, foggy night. Wondering where he was and if he was cold and lonely—and maybe even terribly frightened. She didn't like to think about people being terribly frightened. Particularly not since last November when she'd found out what it was like. She was shivering when she came in, and not just with the cold. As she picked up the phone, Caroline smiled and said, "The usual," which of course meant that it was Melanie.

"April? Hi." Melanie's voice was excited. "I found out."

"Found out? How? When?"

"Just now. In the dictionary. You know. About 'ethical dilemmas.' "

For a moment April couldn't imagine what she was talking about, but then she remembered. "Oh. I thought you meant"—she glanced toward her grandmother, who was reading the paper only a few feet away—"something else."

Melanie understood. "Oh, like where Toby is? No, 'fraid not. Wish I had." She sighed. "But I did find out what his father meant when he said he didn't want to cause an 'ethical dilemma.' I looked it up. 'Ethical' means it has to do with what's *right* and what's *wrong*, and a 'dilemma' is—"

April thought she knew. "A mess," she interrupted. "Doesn't it mean some kind of big messy problem?"

"Right. A big messy problem that there's no good way out of. So an 'ethical dilemma' is the kind of problem that whatever answer you choose, it's not a good choice. Like when you have to choose"—Melanie lowered her voice—"between lying or breaking a promise. Get it?"

"Yeah, I get it." April didn't dare discuss it under the circumstances, but she knew exactly what Melanie was referring to at that particular moment. Like when Toby's dad asked you if you'd seen Toby since he'd left home.

"Well, I guess you can't talk much at the moment?" Melanie, as usual, guessed correctly.

"Right. That's right. I can't."

"Okay. Guess it will wait till—" Melanie was beginning to say when April interrupted.

"No. No it won't," she said. She couldn't explain. Not with Caroline sitting right there in the room. She couldn't say that she absolutely had to talk to someone about the things she'd been thinking out there on the balcony or else she'd have nightmares again for sure. Talking to Caroline had helped a lot lately with the dark-alley nightmares, but right now talking to any adult about Toby was impossible. So the only other possibility was to talk to Melanie.

"Uh, look," April went on, "do you still have . . ." She thought quickly. "Do you still have that book?"

"Which book?"

"The one about Gypsies. You know. The long one Mrs. George found for us."

"Yeah," Melanie said. "It's still here. Why?"

"Why do you think, silly? I want to read it. Could I come down and get it?"

"Right now? It's pretty late."

"I know. I won't stay very long. I just want to get the book."

Melanie said she thought that would be okay and so did Caroline, as long as April didn't stay more than five minutes. April started down to the second floor, thinking about what she wanted to say to Melanie and the kinds of helpful ideas she hoped Melanie would have.

But when she knocked on the Rosses' door, Melanie met her in the entry hall with the thick book about Gypsies already in her hand. "Here it is," she said. "My mom said we can't talk very long. I haven't finished my homework."

"Look. Could I come in for just a minute?" April asked. "I've got to talk to you. It's about . . . Well, it's about Toby."

"What about Toby?"

April came in and closed the door behind her. "Well, the thing is, we've just got to *do* something. I mean, right away. I mean, I keep thinking about where he is and what might be happening, and I keep getting these pictures in my head and I can't get them out. Pictures about something happening to him like what almost happened to me. I just feel like—well, we just have to do something *right away*."

Melanie looked at April thoughtfully for a moment before she said, "I guess the only thing we could do right now—I mean, right this minute—is to tell."

"Tell?" April was shocked. "Tell who?"

"Our folks. And the police too, I guess. Because if we tell our folks, they'll tell the police, for sure."

"But we can't," April said. "We promised."

Melanie nodded knowingly. "Like I said, it's an ethical dilemma."

April sighed impatiently. Just being told that you were in an ethical dilemma didn't help all that much. Not with nightmares anyway. So she was already feeling frustrated when Melanie kind of shoved the book into her hands. "There it is. I have to go. Did you really want to read it?"

That did it. "Sure," April said in a tight, carefully controlled voice. "I said I did, didn't I? You think I was lying?"

"No. I thought . . . Oh, I don't know. It seemed to me that . . ." Melanie took a deep breath. "It just seems like the whole Gypsy thing isn't working very well."

There it was again. There Melanie was, doing a downer about being Gypsies. April's nervous tension suddenly exploded into anger. "Oh, I get it," she said. "You never have liked changing to Gypsies, and I know why. I mean, just because it was my idea in the first place you never have— you keep on—you just . . ." Staring at Melanie, watching the way her big dark eyes widened and then narrowed as if she was in pain, April stammered to a stop.

A moment later she sighed deeply, and then went on, "I didn't mean . . . That is, what I meant was . . . I know the Gypsy thing hasn't exactly happened yet. Not like Egypt did anyway. But it would have if all that other stuff

129

hadn't come up. You know, like Bear showing up and then Toby disappearing and . . ." She threw up her hands.

Melanie nodded. "I know," she said. "That's part of it. Bear and Toby and everything are part of it. But that's not all." She was twisting her hands together the way she sometimes did when she was upset. "And you know it's not fair saying that I didn't want to be a Gypsy because it was your idea."

April grinned sarcastically. "There you go again. Old Melanie 'That's-Not-Fair' Ross."

Melanie's answering smile was almost real, but then she shrugged and went on. "Well, it's not. You know I really liked the Gypsy idea at first. And when we were finding out all those things about caravans and costumes and traveling around telling fortunes and training animals and that kind of stuff. I really liked that part. It's just that . . ." She was wringing her hands again. "Well, some of it's in there." She pointed at the book April was holding. "There. In that book."

April looked down at the big fat book in her hands. Turning it over, she looked at the title. *The Eternal Outcasts* by someone with a strange, unpronounceable name. "What do you mean, it's in this book?"

"Why the game didn't work very well. At least for me," Melanie said. "I mean, what happens to Gypsies is too . . . I don't know." She shrugged and made her face say something like, "I know what you're going to say, and I don't care," before she went on. "It's just not—*fair*."

April couldn't believe it. "Look, Ross," she said, tight-lipped and boiling-over angry. "Would you please knock off that 'not fair' business for a minute or two. I'm getting so sick of all that goody-goody stuff that I could—"

But at that moment Melanie's mom came into the living room and said, "Okay, girls. Time's up. School day tomorrow."

Giving Melanie a final disgusted glare, April slammed the door behind her before she dashed up the stairs.

At one o'clock the next morning she was still reading *The Eternal Outcasts*. She had read about how Gypsies were, for hundreds of years, an outcast people who were never allowed to settle in one place and then were punished for being wanderers. And who were not allowed to own land or work at ordinary jobs and then were persecuted because they lived by their wits. She read about places where the laws had said it wasn't a crime to kill a Gypsy and about countries where Gypsies had been arrested on sight to be beaten or even killed and where Gypsies had even been slaves to be bought and sold. And then, more recently, how Hitler and the Nazis had sent half a million Gypsies to die in the gas chambers. It was almost one-thirty when she finally threw the book down, turned out the light, and lay staring wide-eyed into the darkness.

There was no use shutting her eyes because she wasn't going to sleep. She probably wasn't going to sleep all night long. She sighed and thumped her pillow with her fist. Here she'd gone down to talk to Melanie, who was supposed to be her friend, because she was feeling really rotten and needed to be cheered up, and look what happened. *Thanks a lot, Melanie.*

And besides, she really didn't believe that reading that

stupid book was why Melanie stopped wanting to be a Gypsy. Sure there were a lot of unfair things in it, but so what? There were probably a lot of unfair things that happened to ancient Egyptians, too. There were a lot of unfair things everywhere. Everywhere! Like having a mother who didn't want you around, so you got sent off to live with your grandmother. What was so fair about that? She punched the pillow again, harder. Then she punched it with both fists and began to cry.

Somehow the crying helped. The pillow had just started to get wet when she began to feel sleepy.

Nineteen

IT WAS BAD enough to fall, almost headfirst, into a mysterious hole under an old abandoned church, but that was just the beginning. Toby had no more than caught his balance and staggered to a stop when a match flared in the darkness and a strange, creaky voice said something about an ugly monster. That did it. His heart immediately began to thunder somewhere near the roof of his mouth. He tried to swallow it back down to where it belonged, but it stayed put, and when he turned around to run, he found that his legs seemed to be out of control too. Except for one or two wobbly steps, nothing much happened.

Meanwhile a candle flamed in the darkness, and then another. The match was shaken out, and the creaky voice spoke again. "Well, well. And another visitor. Who have we here, Bruno? Who's your handsome young friend?"

Then, suddenly, he recognized the speaker. The strange crackly voice first, and then, even in the faint candlelight, the puckered old face and masses of dirty white hair. It was Garbo, the ragged old beggar woman who had been hanging out in doorways on University Avenue ever since last spring. Everyone who lived in the area had seen her, but no one seemed to know who she was or what her real name was or where she disappeared to every night. Not even the people like Toby's dad, who always put money in her cup whenever he had any to spare, and sometimes even when he didn't. Toby had seen him drop what was just about his last dollar bill in her cup. Always the same big tin cup with a chipped and faded picture of Greta Garbo on it.

"Hi, G-G-Garbo," Toby stammered as soon as he could get the words out over the lump of throbbing terror that still seemed to be stuck in the back of his throat.

She nodded, her eyes narrowing suspiciously. "Who are you, boy? What's your name?"

"Tob—" he started to say before he changed his mind and, fishing around desperately, came up with Tony. "Tony," he said. "My name's Tony J-J-Johnson."

Garbo smiled slyly, showing a scattering of teeth in mostly empty gums. Toby could see now that she was sitting in a pile of blankets and mattresses in a kind of alcove beside a bulky metallic shape that looked as if it had once been a furnace. "Well, well, so it's Tony J-J-Johnson," she chuckled. "What brings you to my private abode at this hour of the night?"

"What b-brings m-me . . ." Toby paused, gulped, and then stumbled on, making stuff up as he went along. Making up what he thought at first was a pretty good story, considering the fact that he had absolutely no time to work on it. "Well, see, it's l-l-like this. I'm k-k-kind of an escapee from an orphan home." He thought that was a nice touch. He had a feeling Garbo could relate to orphans.

"An escapee orphan?" Garbo asked. "They got an orphanage in this town?"

He wasn't too sure about that, so just to be on the safe side, he changed his plot a little. "Well, I haven't been an orphan very long." He was pleased to find that his voice had stopped shaking. "I just lost my parents recently. Just last week, in fact."

"That recently." Garbo nodded seriously.

He went on then, telling about how his parents had mysteriously disappeared and he had to run away because the police were going to put him in a terrible orphanage where kids were whipped and tortured and fed on bread and water. Before he'd finished, he began to realize that the story had some major holes in it, but it didn't seem to matter, since by then Garbo seemed to have lost interest. While he was talking, she was either fiddling with her fingerless gloves or pawing among the blankets as if she were looking for something. He was just getting to an especially good part when she interrupted.

"Bruno," she said. "Come here and say hello."

"Bruno" was definitely what she said, but it was Bear who trotted over. Up until that moment he'd been sniffing around in a dark corner of the basement and whining softly to himself, but when Garbo called him, he came immediately. But gently. Very gently, for Bear. Instead of bouncing all over her as he did when he greeted other people, he crept over quietly, lay down beside her, and put his head in her lap.

"So, Bruno," she said, scratching his head. "So you've gone out and found yourself another big-time phony to take up with. And poor old Jeb not cold in his grave." She looked up at Toby, a slicing sideways glance. "So you followed Bruno here?"

But Toby's throat was tightening again. Garbo went back to petting Bear, who, it seemed, was also known as Bruno.

135

But who was poor old Jeb, and what had happened to him? Toby gulped and asked, "Who is—was Jeb?"

Garbo chuckled. "Yes, who *was* Jeb is right, I'm afraid. Dead now. Old friend of mine. Died in his sleep, right over there in that corner where he and Bruno used to hang out. Happened just a few days ago. And right after they took Jeb away, Bruno here just up and disappears. Thought they'd taken him away to the doggy gas chambers, I did." Bending over Bear, she picked up his ear and whispered, "Glad to see you gave 'em the slip, sweetie." She petted and crooned for a little longer before she suddenly looked up at Toby.

"Well, well, Tony J-J-Johnson," she said. "Make yourself at home, dearie. Gets pretty cold in here nights. Hope you've got some blankets in that pack of yours." She looked toward the area where Bear had been sniffing. "I'd offer you some of Jeb's, but it looks like the other boys already latched on to them."

"The—the other boys?" Toby looked around nervously. "Who . . ."

"My other roomers," Garbo said. "Out working at the moment. Vince and Mickey. Nice boys, both of them. Have a few problems, of course." She chuckled again, a laugh that somehow managed to sound like what people do when someone tells a very unfunny joke. "A few little problems fate dealt them, like a slipped cog or two. And killer headaches. Not a bit dangerous, though . . ." Her sly smile came back as she added, "At least not very often."

Toby found himself backing away.

"You aren't thinking of leaving me, are you, dearie?" Garbo asked. "Seems to me you'd be better off to stay here at least for tonight. Streets aren't a good place for a young fellow like you, nowadays. 'Specially at night."

"I know," Toby said, "but I think I'd better go anyway. At least for now. Maybe I'll come back later." He turned to go, but when Bear came bouncing after him, he stopped to look back.

"That's right," Garbo said. "If you must go, take the dog. Great ugly beast like that might discourage some of the other beasts out there. Go on now, but do come back if you find you have to. Remember that, dearie. You can come back if you have to."

"Thanks. Thanks a lot. Maybe I will," Toby said again, but he certainly didn't mean it. No way he'd ever go back down into that disgusting dark hole where poor old crazy Garbo, and who knew how many other weirdos, hung out. "Fat chance," he muttered as he started off down Arbor Street.

Hanging on to Bear's fur almost all the way, and fighting off several major panic attacks, he made it as far as the After Hours Club without meeting anyone who showed any interest in him. But, sure enough, not far from that run-down bar he had to pass another bunch of mean-looking guys, who started following along behind him and kept on following for the next couple of blocks. Maybe it was the sight of Bear that discouraged them as Garbo had predicted, but for whatever reason they eventually turned off into a parking lot. Afterward, Toby told himself that the good news was that he didn't have to worry that those creeps had recognized him and would tell the police about seeing the missing Alvillar kid, because they obviously weren't the

137

type who talked to police officers. Not unless they had to, anyway.

That trip back down Arbor was pretty bad, but there was one change for the better, which was that this time Bear stayed right beside him without even once trying to pull away. It was as if he'd been so stubborn before because he was just so determined to find out whether or not his old friend had come back. He hadn't, of course, and according to Garbo, he wasn't about to. Maybe Bear knew that now and maybe he didn't, but for whatever reason he seemed willing to follow wherever his new friend wanted to go. So that left only one problem. The new friend didn't have the faintest idea where he was going.

So even though he really couldn't say that it had been Bear's decision this time, it really hadn't been his, either. At least not as far as he could remember. Not the kind that you make with your brain anyway. But some part of him, his feet probably, had automatically turned onto Norwich and then into the alley that led toward Orchard Avenue. And a little later, probably pretty close to ten o'clock, Toby and Bear turned into the passageway between the Gypsy Camp and the Casa Rosada, squeezed in through the loose plank, and curled up together on the crib mattress, behind the caravan mural.

Twenty

TOBY DIDN'T SLEEP much that night. Although he was pretty comfortable, curled up with Bear on the old crib mattress, things kept waking him up. It wasn't just the fleas, either. Actually, he was getting kind of used to them. Once it was the scream of a police siren, and another time it was a faint ghostly noise that seemed to be coming from the alley beyond the high board fence. And now and then it was just Bear, having a lively paw-twitching dream. Finally, in the wee hours of the morning, Toby gave up on sleeping and began to do some serious thinking. That turned out to be a big mistake. Serious thinking at that time of night usually is.

As soon as he gave his brain the green light, it turned traitor and began to torment him with a long parade of scary facts. Facts like how likely it was that the police, or whoever it was who had been right outside the gate with Ken yesterday, would be coming back again today. And how, even if they didn't, the other Gypsies undoubtedly would. And how there just wasn't any way that one of them, or all of them, for that matter, would be able to keep their mouths shut for very long. And, the most tormenting possibility of all, the things that would probably happen if he got caught and forced to go back home.

And all the facts led to just one conclusion: he was going to have to leave the old storage-yard hideout and go somewhere else. But where? And also, how soon? He'd had about all he could take of late-night streets, so it would have to be in the morning, in spite of the danger of being seen by people who might recognize him. Being around people was dangerous when you were a fugitive, but after considerable thought, Toby decided that a lot of hurrying people might not be as dangerous as a few curious passersby. During the rush hour, then, might be best, when the streets and sidewalks were crowded and most people were in too much of a hurry to notice who might be scurrying along beside them. That, he decided, would have to be it.

The sky was just beginning to go from black to gray when Toby got up, stuffed most of the old blankets inside his backpack, and said good-bye to Bear. And this time, when he slipped out through the swinging plank, he was very careful to shove it firmly back into place. Shoved and pounded while on the other side of the fence, Bear was scratching and whining pitifully.

"Wish I could take you along, you old four-legged heating pad," Toby whispered as he pounded, "but you wouldn't like it if I did. No kibble where I'm going. And besides, if you disappear, poor old Marshall would just about come unglued." The sounds of scratching and whining followed him as he set off down the alley through the early-morning fog.

At about the time that Toby was telling Bear good-bye, not far away on the third floor of the Casa Rosada, April was

140

waking up and remembering what had happened the night before. Remembering Toby lost out there in the dark, dangerous city and, as if that weren't bad enough, remembering her quarrel with Melanie. How could she face spending the day at school, worrying about Toby and also worrying about the fact that Melanie wasn't speaking to her? Pulling the covers over her head, she tried to go back to sleep, but of course she couldn't. As soon as she closed her eyes, her mind not only started reruns of last night's horror stories about what might have happened to Toby but also threw in some depressing new scenes of Melanie tossing her head, turning her back, and walking away whenever April tried to talk to her.

Finally she pulled the covers down far enough to peek out at the clock on the bedside table, and sighed deeply. Just as she'd feared, it was time to get up. Unless—unless maybe she was sick. She checked out the possibilities. Sore throat? Nothing noticeable. Headache? No luck there either.

Stomachache? Yeah, that was it. Ulcers, probably. Wasn't that what you got from worrying too much? After last night she probably had half a dozen. But after several minutes of concentrating on her stomach, and even giving it a few good hard pokes to help get things started, she gave up on ulcers, too. Crawling out of bed, she stumbled gloomily out into the kitchen.

Caroline, who was rushing around getting breakfast ready, didn't seem to notice that anything was wrong. Didn't even see that something was bothering April. *Just what you could expect from someone who was only a grandmother, instead of a real parent,* April thought, with growing annoyance. *A person might think that at a time like this even a grandmother would notice something, might pay some attention to what her only granddaughter was going through.* April pulled up a chair and threw herself despairingly into it.

But then, when Caroline finally stopped dashing around and sat down at the table, she suddenly began to get terribly nosy. Began to ask all sorts of questions about Toby's disappearance and what people at school were saying about it and how she, April, felt about it. *Just what you'd expect,* April told herself, letting her eyes go narrow and her jaw tighten. *Just like a grandmother. Always prying into people's personal feelings about things.* And then, when April was starting to point out that a person's feelings were sometimes very private and personal, Caroline looked at the clock and said she hoped that April would cheer up soon, and hurried off to work. *Cheer up!* April thought angrily. *As if I was in a bad mood or something.*

Feeling a little bit nervous and worried—but not in a bad mood—April finished getting ready and started down the stairs, still trying to decide whether to ring the Rosses' doorbell and give Melanie a chance to refuse to speak to her. Or whether to just go on to school without her. That's what she ought to do. She ought to just walk on past and . . .

"Hi," a voice said, and there she was. There Melanie was, sitting in the window seat on the first-floor landing.

"Hi, yourself," April said warily, not wanting to sound too relieved or anything. That was all anybody said for a while. It wasn't until they were out on the sidewalk that April said, "Hey, I thought you weren't going to be speaking to me."

"Oh yeah?" Melanie looked surprised. "Why? I mean, why'd you think that?"

April grinned and shrugged. All she said was, "I don't know. No good reason, I guess." But what she was thinking was, *Because I wouldn't be speaking to me, if I were you.*

So that was that. Not really the end of straightening out the Gypsy problem, of course, but pretty much the end of thinking and talking about it for a while. But not the end of worrying about Toby. In class that day it was hard for April to keep her mind on what was going on, and she knew Melanie was having the same problem. Once during math class April had to ask Mrs. Granger to repeat the question, and the same thing happened to Melanie a little while later. Every time they looked at each other, they made desperate faces, looks that meant stuff like, "The day is lasting forever," and "How can you concentrate on uncommon denominators when your mind is full of questions about matters of life or death?" Questions like, "Was Toby really there yesterday when Ken knocked on the gate?" And, "If not, when did he leave?" And, "Where did he spend the night?" And, "What horrible things might have happened to him?" The hours crept slowly by.

When Toby left the Gypsy Camp that morning in the first half-light of day, he really didn't have any idea where he was going except perhaps to quickly get to a different neighborhood where he would be less apt to run into someone he knew. At first he headed west, away from the Wilson School District, but he hadn't gone far when he realized that he was getting too close to University Avenue

143

and home. So at the next corner he turned north and ran into a bunch of hurrying commuters headed for the rapid transit terminal. And since no one in the crowd seemed the least bit interested in him, he stayed with them as far as the Norwich stop. At that point he mingled with the Norwich pedestrians.

He was still hurrying down Norwich trying to look like an ordinary student headed for an ordinary early-morning study hour, or perhaps a before-school music lesson, when he suddenly realized what he had to do. Part of his decision was because of the weather, which was getting darker and gloomier by the minute and threatening the kind of rain that would pretty much rule out any outdoor-living-type solution to his problem. But an even more important deciding factor was pure and simple exhaustion. Suddenly and totally, he was major-league wiped out. Which wasn't too surprising considering the amount of sleep he hadn't been getting. And it was right then, just as he was beginning to realize that he wasn't going to be able to go much farther, when he looked up and noticed that he was about to cross Arbor Street.

She did invite me back, he told himself, as he started up Arbor. *And I won't stay long. Just long enough to get some sleep and decide on a plan of action.*

It was a weird kind of relief to have a plan, even a fairly disgusting one, and to at least know where he was going, but when he reached the church and the steps that led down to the basement, the fear and dread came back in full force. It wasn't until he'd taken off his backpack and fished around for his flashlight that he could force himself to go on down. He pushed open the door and then froze, crouched and ready to run, while he shone the light around the dark recesses of the basement.

They were asleep. All of them. A mound of blankets in Garbo's alcove by the dead furnace was producing the reassuring sound of deep, steady snoring. But there were two other mounds of scruffy blankets, from which there occasionally arose other sleep-related noises, gasps and gurgles and heavy breathing. Standing just inside the door, Toby turned the flashlight from one to the other and then back again, but no one woke up or even moved, and suddenly he was just too tired to go on being afraid. A few minutes later he had spread his blankets in an unoccupied corner, had rolled up in them as best he could, and was rapidly falling asleep. The last thing he remembered thinking was that it was entirely possible that he could wake up dead, but right at that moment he was just too tired to care.

Twenty-one

AS IT TURNED OUT, when Toby woke up a couple of hours later, he wasn't exactly dead, but pretty close to it if you count being scared half to death. If you count being jarred out of a deep, sound sleep by someone pulling your backpack out from under your head, and then just squatting there grinning at you like some kind of weird gargoyle.

Actually, when Toby's head crashed down off his backpack pillow, the person he found himself staring at was just one of Garbo's roommates. A weird old-young guy, with pale white skin and greenish blond hair that stuck out in every direction, and several layers of ragged clothing draping his huge, clumsy-looking body. It was his face that reminded Toby of a gargoyle. Not that he was all that ugly, because he wasn't, but there was something gargoylelike about his empty-eyed, snaggle-toothed, permanent grin. It was the kind of grin that probably wouldn't change a bit while he robbed you and then beat you to a bloody pulp.

"Hi," the gargoyle said, holding up the backpack. "I got your pack." He gave it a shake and then held it up to his ear as if he expected it to say something. "Got some breakfast in there?"

"B-Breakfast?" Toby stammered. "No. No breakfast." But then, as his sleep-dazed brain got into gear, he decided on another answer. "I might have some bread, though. Would you like a piece of bread?"

"Yeah." The grin widened. "Oh boy, oh boy, bread. Mickey likes bread." He nodded happily, and as he handed over the backpack, he added, "I'm Mickey. I live here."

Toby thought of saying, "Yeah, I was afraid of that," but instead he only nodded and pretended to smile as he unzipped the pack and took out the last food bag. All that was left was a fairly well petrified piece of what used to be sourdough French bread. "Here," he said, holding it out to Mickey. "That's it. That's all I've got left."

"Oh boy, oh boy," Mickey said. "Bread." He began to gnaw at the stale bread, using teeth at the side of his mouth because some of the front ones seemed to be rotted out, but then, suddenly, his big smooth face wrinkled into a worried frown. "Where's your piece?" he asked. "Where's your bread?"

Toby shrugged and shook his head. "That's okay. I don't want any. I don't . . ."

But Mickey's worried pucker stayed in place. "Here," he said. "Mickey bust it. Give you some."

The bread didn't break easily. Mickey looked pretty tough, but obviously a really stale chunk of French bread was tougher. He was still grunting and twisting, and Toby was still saying, "No, no, that's all right. I'm not hungry. I'm—" when another voice interrupted.

A harsh, brittle voice that said, "Give it here, Mickey." And suddenly another of Garbo's roommates was standing behind Mickey, holding a long, sharp, murderous-looking knife. Toby gasped and tried to keep his hands from creeping up toward his throat.

147

"Hi, kid," said the guy with the knife, a tall, thin black man with dark brown skin and lots of wild-looking hair. "I'm Vince. And this lamebrain is Mickey." He held out his other hand, the one that wasn't holding the knife. "Here lamebrain, let me."

Toby couldn't help tensing himself to jump out of the way when the fight started. Calling a very large, powerful-looking person a lamebrain was really asking for it, particularly when the person you were talking to obviously was one. And even though Vince was the one with the knife, Mickey was an awful lot bigger. But to Toby's surprise, Mickey only smiled his sappy smile and handed the French bread to Vince, who started sawing a chunk off one end. But as Vince sawed, Toby began to get the picture. What he got was that although the dictionary definition of "lamebrain" might be insulting, Vince's tone of voice hadn't been. And it was pretty obvious that dictionary definitions weren't the kind of thing Mickey worried about. When a smallish piece finally came off the chunk of bread, Vince handed it to Toby and gave the rest back to Mickey.

"Hey, thanks," Toby managed to say, trying to look as though he meant it. As if he really was thrilled to get a small, slobbered-on piece of what was really his in the first place. And in a way he was. At least he was certainly glad that bread seemed to be the only thing Vince showed any interest in slicing up.

Vince's smile, unlike Mickey's permanent grin, was brief and pointed. "Don't worry," he said. "He doesn't have anything catching. Not that I know of anyhow."

Back in his corner, Vince pulled on some old scruffy boots, smoothed his blankets, and gathered up some boxes and plastic bags, while Mickey watched every move he made. Mickey watched Vince's movements the way a normal person might watch some kind of artistic performance, looking back now and then and grinning delightedly, as if he were inviting Toby to share his admiration for his friend's incredible talents. Neither of the two guys said anything more. But, a few minutes later as he was leading Mickey toward the basement door, Vince did a kind of good-bye gesture in Toby's direction. And Mickey, who was still gnawing away, stopped long enough to wave his bread in a kind of eager-beaver imitation of Vince's super-cool salute.

As soon as they were out of sight, Toby started to toss his slimy piece of bread into a dark corner, but at the last moment he changed his mind. It was a depressing thought, but just because he wasn't desperate enough to eat a rock-hard, slightly-chewed-on chunk of bread at the moment didn't mean that he might not be that desperate sometime in the future. He was stuffing it back into his backpack, when a familiar creaky voice said, "Well, well. The return of Mr. J-J-Johnson. And I see you've already met our fellow cellar rats."

Toby smiled weakly. "Yeah, I guess so. Is that—er—all of them?" He hoped it was. He didn't know if he could take any more Vinces or Mickeys at the moment.

Garbo was sitting up among her jumble of blankets. "That's it. Just the three of us poor outcasts, since Jeb died." She grinned teasingly. "Four again, come to think of it, with our new young recruit. Tony, you said? Come here, Tony, and help me get on my feet."

Toby-Tony did as he was told, and by the time he'd

149

helped Garbo gather up her blankets and climb the stairs, he'd learned quite a lot more about Garbo and her fellow cellar rats. Like for instance the fact that both Vince and Mickey had been in institutions at one time.

"Institutions?" That didn't sound too reassuring. "What kind of institutions? You don't mean like—like they're crazy, or something?"

Garbo chuckled. "No, not crazy. At least Mickey isn't. 'Fraid poor old Mickey doesn't have what it takes to go crazy." When Toby just stared at her in bewilderment, she went on, "In this stark raving world of ours, it's usually the ones who started out with a certain amount of smarts who eventually freak out and flip their everlasting lids. That's definitely not our Mickey's problem. His gears are just missing a few cogs."

"And Vince?" Toby asked, remembering the sharp, fierce eyes, and the wicked knife.

"Vince? Crazy? No. Not exactly. Didn't used to be, at least. Guess old Vince used to be some kind of businessman, believe it or not. But then a few years ago his head got kind of smashed in, and ever since then he gets these terrible, blinding headaches. Real doozies! Drives him right up the wall sometimes. Lost his job, and the doctors took all his money."

"Wow," Toby said. "That's a bummer. Does his head ache like that all the time?"

"No. Not all the time." Garbo shook her head. "They come and go. But sometimes they last for days. Mickey takes care of him when he's out of it, or he'd probably have been dead by now. And the rest of the time Vince takes care of Mickey." Garbo laughed her unfunny laugh. "They're quite a pair. Good roommates, though. Except you don't want to go messing with Vince when his head's bad. Times like that he's got a pretty short fuse."

They were out on the path by then, and before she left, Garbo showed Toby where it was possible to get water from a faucet behind the liquor store and the way to something she called "Jeb's sanitary facility," which was a makeshift outhouse that her old friend, Jeb, had built in the midst of some bushes in the backyard of the church. Then she warned him again to stay off the streets and set out at a slow shuffle toward downtown.

Toby got a drink, used the sanitary facility, which was anything but sanitary and smelled awful, and then sat on the back steps for a while trying not to notice what a dark and gloomy day it was. Trying not to think at all, actually. The trouble with thinking in a situation like this, he decided, was that as soon as you got started on a useful train of thought, you got sidetracked onto something else. Something useless and completely depressing, like where your dad was right at that moment and what he was doing and how he was feeling. *Just don't think about it*, he told himself firmly. *Concentrate on something useful, like planning what you're going to do next, for instance.*

But then, as soon as he started to make plans about where to go and what to do, he got sidetracked again onto the risks involved in going anywhere, and the maybe even greater danger of staying where he was. The danger of staying in a cold, damp, dirty basement full of crazies and lamebrains, where you would never know when you might

151

be tromped on for not having any more food in your backpack or maybe even knifed by a guy with an extra-bad headache.

The next sidetrack was about food. Just thinking about all the great stuff the other kids had shown up with, the doughnuts and egg rolls and apples and cheese and bread, made him swallow hard. If only he'd rationed it out, leaving at least one doughnut and maybe some cheese and bread for today. But he hadn't, of course. He'd wolfed most of it down immediately, back in the storage yard, and the rest of it, except for that one chunk of stale bread, in his cement-pipe fox hole. Thinking about bread made him remember the small, slobbery chunk in his backpack, but he wasn't quite desperate enough for that yet. Almost, but not quite.

Thinking, Toby decided, was just too depressing, and under the circumstances there was only one way to stop doing it. Returning to the dark, cold basement, he crawled into his rat's nest of blankets and went back to sleep.

Twenty-two

WHEN SCHOOL WAS finally over that day, April and Melanie met Elizabeth outside the fourth-grade room and headed for home—walking fast. But they'd only gone a block or two when there was the whir of wheels and a bicycle whizzed past barely missing them, and then screeched to a stop. Elizabeth squealed in terror, and all three girls leaped for safety. Plastered against the wall of the nearest building, they turned to look—at Ken, of course.

"Hi," he said. "Don't forget. Be there"—he looked at his watch—"in ten minutes."

"You jerk!" April yelled. "Don't you know it's against the law to ride on the sidewalk? Don't you know you could kill . . ."

Melanie was pulling on April's sleeve and shushing her, and when April finally wound down, Melanie said, "We can't. We can't be there in ten minutes. Besides, I don't even know if I can be there at all. We have to pick up Marshall and then I have to get permission and then . . ."

Ken looked disgusted. "Okay, okay." He jumped back on his bike and started off, calling back over his shoulder, "Just get there as soon as you can. We've got to start right away."

That's when they began to run the rest of the way to the

day-care center, breaking all existing records. After they picked up Marshall, he slowed them down some until April and Melanie decided to take his hands and pull him along between them as they ran. It worked pretty well, but it turned out that Marshall didn't like it. He didn't complain while they were running, but when they finally got to the Casa Rosada and April asked, "Wasn't that fun, Marshall?" he jerked his hands away and said, "No!"

"Why not?" Melanie asked. "Did we hurt you?"

Marshall shook his head thoughtfully. "Not hurt. Dragged. You dragged me!" he said, and stomped up the stairs.

As it turned out, getting permission to go to the Gypsy Camp wasn't much of a problem after all. To Melanie's surprise, her mother seemed to have stopped worrying about kidnappers because of an article in the morning paper. And because of another article, she now seemed to be more worried about rain. While her mother was in the kitchen fixing Marshall's honey and peanut butter afternoon sandwich, Melanie snuck in a quick call to April. The line was busy at first, but then April answered.

"Hey," Melanie said. "Your phone's been busy."

"Yeah, I called Caroline. You know, about going to the Gypsy Camp. She said okay as long as I wear my raincoat."

Melanie laughed. "That's just what my mom said. My mom says the paper said there'd be rain, and"—Melanie's voice dropped to a whisper—"and a lot of new stuff about Toby."

"Yeah, that's what Caroline said too. About how the police have decided that there's reason to believe that Toby just ran away, instead of being kidnapped, or any other foul play kind of stuff."

"Right," Melanie said. "I guess that's what it said. So we can go to the Gypsy Camp, as long as we all stay together. My mom sounded pretty relieved."

"Caroline was relieved too, I guess," April said. "But she's still awful worried about Toby. And curious. Caroline is major-league curious about the whole thing. She kept asking me if I had any idea why Toby would run away."

"My folks are the same way," Melanie said. "My mom thinks we should have noticed that something was bothering Toby. Last night she kept asking about that day we were all in Toby's dad's studio. And they really freaked when I told them what it looked like. My dad said he's heard some pretty weird rumors about Toby's dad from some people who used to know him when he was in graduate school."

"What rumors?" April asked.

Melanie shook her head. "I asked him, but he wouldn't tell me. But it was about something that happened a long time ago, back when Toby was a real little kid."

It was just then that Mrs. Ross came into the room, followed by Marshall, who was still chewing on his last mouthful of honey and peanut butter. Mrs. Ross reminded Melanie that she'd promised that they'd all stay together. "And don't forget your rain gear," she added.

"Yeah," Marshall said in a sticky voice. "Don't forget boots."

Melanie had gotten Marshall into his new yellow slicker by the time April came down the stairs, but they were still arguing about which boots he was going to wear. "But those ones match," he was saying, pointing to their mom's yellow boots.

"They're way too big," April said. "What if we have to run? You can't run fast enough in big boots like that."

Marshall grinned. "Yes I can," he said. "If you drag me. If we have to run fast, I'll let you drag me. Okay?"

At that point Melanie gave up arguing and went back in to ask her mother about the boots, and then they still had to put them on him and stop by for Elizabeth. So it was an awful lot more than Ken's ten minutes before they were finally on their way.

They were going down the front steps of the Casa Rosada when Elizabeth asked Melanie if she'd told her folks about the policemen who'd been looking for Toby. And without stopping to think about Marshall being right there listening to everything, Melanie said, "Well, I told them that some policemen had talked to us, but I didn't say where exactly. I didn't mention that they actually came inside the Gypsy Camp because . . ." At that point she happened to see the look on Marshall's face and stopped in midsentence. But it was too late.

Marshall, who had been stomping along happily in the big yellow boots, stopped stomping and stared at Melanie, his big eyes wide and accusing. "Policemen?" he asked. "In the Gypsy Camp? Did they see Bear? Did they take him to the pound?" Marshall's face was beginning to look like one of the sad masks actors wore in the ancient Greek plays. Grabbing Melanie's arm, he began to shake it. "Did they?" he howled. "Did they take my Bear to the pound?"

It wasn't easy to calm Marshall down and convince him

that Bear was all right. That the kind of policemen who looked for missing kids usually weren't interested in stray dogs. Or bears either. Especially not bears! But Marshall wasn't buying it. He started to run, falling over his big boots every few steps and howling at the top of his lungs. He went right on howling until they got to the gate, unlocked it, and shoved it open. And there Bear was, bouncing around, licking faces, and nearly knocking people down, as usual.

Ken was already at the Gypsy Camp all right, sitting on the edge of the shed floor, holding a Domenico's Deli bag on his lap. He was frowning, but when Melanie asked him if he'd been waiting long, he just shrugged and said, "Not all that long. I had to go to the deli first."

"To the deli?" April asked. "Why?"

"Because I wanted to bring some more food. You know, just in case we find Tobe and he's hungry again." His grin was a little sad. "You know how Tobe is. He gets hungrier than anybody. I was going to raid the refrigerator again, but then I found out my mom was kind of suspicious about all that stuff I brought the other night. So I went to Domenico's instead."

"Humph!" April said, thinking, *You might have told us. You might have said you were going all the way to the deli first, instead of yelling at us to be here in ten lousy minutes.* But since they were already late, she didn't figure they had time for a really good argument. So she only changed the subject by asking Ken if he'd found any clues when he'd looked around last night.

Ken shook his head. "After all of you left, I walked up

157

the alley a couple of blocks and then down the other way. I didn't see anything. But I'm going to look some more now. Are you guys going to help?"

They all said they would help if they could, but what could they do? "There's the whole city," Melanie said, "and he might be anywhere. Where should we start?" She looked up at the gray January sky. "And whatever we do, we've got to do it right away, because it's supposed to start raining pretty soon."

Everybody agreed that they had to start soon, but nobody had any very good ideas about how. Or where. Ken said they ought to split up and go in different directions and then meet back at the Gypsy Camp in one hour, but nobody else thought that made much sense.

"Besides," Melanie said, "we promised we'd stay together."

Ken shrugged, and after that they just stood around thinking and disagreeing about what they ought to do. When April suggested that they could start at the doughnut shop because Toby was so crazy about doughnuts, nobody took her very seriously. But then Elizabeth came up with a slightly more reasonable idea.

"Maybe we could go out through the hole in the fence like Toby did and then . . . and then just use our imaginations."

Ken looked at her suspiciously. "What do you mean, use our imaginations?" Ever since he'd been talked into becoming an ancient Egyptian, Ken had been suspicious of people who went overboard on the imagination bit.

Elizabeth ducked her head and looked embarrassed. "I just meant, we could go out through the fence like he did, and then just stand there and pretend we're Toby and imagine what he might have done next."

Nobody really thought it would work, not even Melanie. But since no one had come up with a better plan, they decided to give it a try. They squeezed out into the alley, one at a time, and started concentrating on being Toby and imagining what he would do. They were concentrating so hard that no one, not even Marshall, noticed what Bear was doing. It wasn't until Bear was out into the alley and running around in circles, that they began to react.

"Bear!" Marshall shrieked. "My Bear's running away."

Twenty-three

"CATCH HIM!" Ken shouted as Bear dashed past. "Grab him." He lunged and missed, and Bear went on running in circles. Then everyone got into the act, grabbing at Bear as he went by, until suddenly Melanie yelled, "Wait! Wait, everyone. Leave him alone. Look what he's doing."

They all saw it then. What Bear was doing was sniffing the ground every once in a while like a bloodhound following a scent: running and stopping and sniffing and then taking off again. Following quietly at a distance, they rounded the corner just in time to see him stopping by a long section of concrete drainage pipe. The same piece of pipe, it occurred to April, that the early Egyptians had once used as a hiding place way back in the beginning of the Egypt Game.

At the pipe Bear stopped, sniffed some more, and began to whine. They stared at each other. "In the pipe," April whispered. "He's hiding in the pipe just like we did. Remember?" Ken pushed Bear out of the way, got down on his hands and knees, and stuck his head into the pipe. After a minute he pulled his head out and stood up. "He's not in there," he said, "but something is. I can't reach it but it looks like . . ."

But April was already wiggling her way into the pipe. It was a tight fit. Ken would never have made it, but Toby might have. A minute later she wiggled back out with a paper bag in her hand, a bag that Melanie immediately recognized.

"That's mine." She grabbed it out of April's hand. "That's from the French bakery where my mom buys our bread. I used it for my food for Toby." Opening the bag, she pulled out a cheese rind and an apple core. There was no doubt about it. It was Melanie's bag. So there wasn't much doubt that Toby had been in the pipe, at least for a while.

The big kids were still examining the paper bag when a hollow-sounding voice echoed and re-echoed. "Toby! To-by! To-by!" It was Marshall on his hands and knees, halfway into the pipe. All you could see of him was his little rear end and his big yellow rain boots. "Toby," Marshall called, and the pipe echoed, "To-by, To-by, To-by."

"Come out of there," Melanie said. "Toby's gone somewhere else."

Ken looked frustrated. "Yeah, but I bet he was in there when I walked right by last night. But he didn't say anything," Ken said.

"Were you calling him or talking or anything?" April asked. When Ken shook his head, she went on, "Because if you weren't, he might not have known it was you. He couldn't have seen you. Not if he went in there headfirst anyway. So he might have just kept quiet till the footsteps went away. And then he probably came out and went somewhere else."

161

"Yeah, obviously," Ken said. "But the question is, where? Where would he go to hide?" He looked up and down the alley before he asked, "Anybody got any ideas?"

Marshall's head was still in the pipe. "Not me," he said, and the pipe echoed, "Not me. Not me. Not me."

Unfortunately Marshall wasn't the only one who didn't have any ideas. As Ken looked from face to face, they tried to think of a good hiding place in the neighborhood, but no one came up with anything. April did suggest the park, but Ken didn't agree at all. "No. The park is pretty dangerous these days, particularly after dark. Toby knows that. He wouldn't go there."

"Well, I guess nobody has any ideas," Melanie said. "Unless . . . unless Bear does." She suddenly began to look around frantically. "Where is Bear?"

No Bear running around everyone in circles. No Bear with Marshall, who was just backing out of the pipe. No Bear . . .

"There he is!" Marshall shouted. "Up there. By the corner."

They all saw him then, trotting along the alley and turning the corner in the direction of Norwich Avenue. In a flash they were all running after him.

Bear could run a lot faster than they could. Even a lot faster than Ken, at least when Ken was carrying a big bag of food. And a lot faster than April and Melanie, who were dragging Marshall between them. They might never have caught up if he hadn't stopped now and then to sniff the ground. He would start sniffing, and they'd almost catch up, but then, when they'd almost reached him, he would be off again, running at top speed. It wasn't until he came out of the alley onto busy Norwich Avenue that Ken managed to catch up with him and grab his collar.

"Got him," he yelled, then as the rest of them straggled up, "Whew! It's a good thing I nabbed him. He might have run right out into the traffic."

"Not—unless—Toby—did," Melanie panted. "If he's following Toby's scent, he'll go wherever Toby did."

"Yeah." April was pretty breathless, too. "Come on, Bear. Let's go. Go find Toby."

But Bear, it seemed, wasn't going anywhere with anybody hanging on to his collar. Instead, he just sat down and looked up at Ken questioningly. The answer was obviously a rope, but that was back in the Gypsy Camp. "Well, I guess someone could go all the way back for the leash," Melanie said. "It would take a lot of time, but I don't know what else we can do unless"—suddenly she stared at Ken—"unless we could use somebody's belt."

"Oh no. Not my Gucci belt," Ken said. "My dad bought it for me. Besides, I need it."

April saw what he meant. Ken's pants, which were fashionably baggy, looked as if they might be a problem without a belt.

A brief argument followed, in which Melanie said that it was certainly a dilemma, but that losing your pants wouldn't be nearly as wrong as letting Bear get lost or even letting him run out into the traffic. And April tactfully pointed out that if a person wore pants that were anywhere near his actual size, a person could get along without a belt, at least in an emergency. At about that point Ken unexpectedly gave up, and a few minutes later they were off again, following Bear down the sidewalk toward the corner of Norwich and Arbor Street. But this time Elizabeth had charge of the Domenico's Deli bag so that Ken could have his left hand free, in case of an emergency.

Norwich was still pretty busy that afternoon, and a lot of people stopped to stare. April didn't see why, even though you might have to admit the five of them and Bear weren't exactly your usual neighborhood gang. Not because they were a lot of different races, either. People in the university area were used to that. Or even that they were different ages and sexes, which was a little more peculiar. There was more to it than that. There was, for instance, Bear himself, an unusually weird-looking black dog who was whining loudly and straining at the end of a wide leather leash, which a large sixth-grade kid was holding with one hand while he held up his pants with the other. A kid who kept stopping to yell back over his shoulder at a bunch of girls, two of whom were dragging a small boy in a yellow slicker and enormous yellow boots.

But there was no reason for people to stop and stare. And certainly no reason to laugh, because it wasn't funny. And April would have told them so right to their faces if she'd been able to stop long enough to do it. But she couldn't because they had to keep up with Bear and Ken. So she just tried to ignore the gawkers, and the good news was that as soon as they turned onto Arbor they were out of the Wilson School District, at least. That meant the people who stopped to stare were much less likely to know who they were.

About two blocks up Arbor Street they reached an area that had once been residential but was now mostly second-hand stores and warehouses. The few old houses that remained standing had been changed into businesses like repair shops and liquor stores. The sidewalk was cracked in places, and there were tall dry weeds beside the curb and in the vacant lots. Ken pulled Bear to a stop and looked around.

"Pretty crummy area, huh?" he said. "Toby wouldn't have come here. I'll bet Bear isn't following Toby's scent anyway. He doesn't even stop to sniff very often. He's probably just trying to go back where he came from. And, if you ask me, that's what we better do. And the sooner the better."

Melanie knew what he meant. It was a neighborhood she was supposed to stay out of. But, on the other hand, she could think of one reason why Toby might have headed this way. "Wait a minute," she said. "He might have come here if he was looking for a place where he wasn't going to see anyone he knows." She paused, and then went on, "And besides—just look at Bear."

Sure enough, Bear was straining at the leash, and his tail was wagging like crazy.

"Well, okay. Just a little farther then," Ken said reluctantly.

A few minutes later Bear raised his head and began to sniff, not the sidewalk, but the air. Whining happily, he took off, dragging Ken behind him down the sidewalk toward an old boarded-up church.

But Bear wasn't interested in the front of the church. Pulling so hard against his collar that he almost choked himself, he dragged Ken past the entryway and down a weed-bordered path that led to the back of the building, with the girls and Marshall following close behind.

165

The path passed some more windows and a boarded-up back entrance and ended at some steps that led down to a basement door. A door that was not only unboarded but was not even entirely closed. Whimpering excitedly, Bear dashed down the steps, pawed open the door, and rushed in, pulling Ken behind him into almost complete darkness.

The air was dank and smelled like mildewed clothing and rotting vegetables. The only light came from a small flickering flame, as if a candle was burning somewhere in the distance. And in the dim candlelight something vague and shadowy was moving. Ken's eyes were still adjusting to the lack of light when a familiar voice said, "Holy cow, Kamata. What are you doing here?"

Twenty-four

THE NEXT FEW minutes were complete confusion. Bear was jumping all over Toby and whimpering with joy, the girls and Marshall were stumbling down the steps into the semidarkness, and Toby was saying, "Hey, Melanie! And April! Down, Bear. Watch it! Don't step on the candle. And Elizabeth too. Hey, and more food. Wow, I sure can use that. Down, boy! Cool it. Watch out for the candle." It wasn't until he picked up the bottle that held the candle, shoved it into Ken's hands; and gave Bear his full attention that things began to settle down.

"Wow," Toby said after he finally got Bear to stop celebrating and lie down, "the gang's all here." Kneeling down, he fussed around, smoothing out some blankets. "Here, sit down, everybody. Pull up a blanket. Hey, Marshall. Great boots, man! Ken, put the candle down here, on this box." Chattering on and on as if he were someplace normal, instead of hiding out like a criminal in the cold, dark, smelly basement of an old abandoned church, in a very dangerous part of town. Chattering away and grinning in an almost convincing way as if everything were okay. Watching Toby's performance, April and Melanie looked at each other and made their eyes say, "I can't believe it." But out loud they were almost speechless, and so were Ken and Elizabeth.

After Toby finally managed to get everyone to sit down, they continued to stare at him in silent amazement. A long awkward moment passed before Toby waved his arms around and said, "Well, what do you think of my new space?" Nobody answered. Toby sighed dramatically. "I know. It's not exactly the Ritz. But it's not always this— this lonely."

Ken finally found his tongue. "What do you mean, 'Not always this lonely'?" He looked around uneasily. "You mean someone else is holed up here?"

"Well, sort of," Toby said, "but not exactly. More like they just live here. But hey, it's all right. They're okay. There's this nice old lady and a couple of other people. Real nice guys, believe it or not."

April didn't believe it. Not in this place. Not in this terrible dark hole. She was anxiously checking out shadowy corners while Toby went on. "Oh, don't worry. Nobody's here now. They're all out—er, working." The almost-real grin was back. "But what I want to know is, how'd you ever find me?"

"Bear found you," a muffled voice said. It was Marshall, whose face was buried in Bear's fuzzy neck.

"Is that right?" Toby sounded amazed.

"Yeah, Bear found you." Ken's voice was angry and so was his face. "Look here, Alvillar. You're the one who has to start answering questions. What do you think you're doing anyway? We've all been going out of our skulls worrying about you. Everybody. The whole school and the neighborhood, and everybody's been freaking out."

"Oh yeah?" Toby looked very interested, almost pleased with himself, as if he were actually enjoying hearing that he was the latest hot-gossip topic. "For real? The whole neighborhood?"

But now April had found her voice, too. "Yeah, and your poor dad is really worried. He's just about to . . ."

Toby's expression changed quickly. "My dad. How do you know? Where did you see my dad? How—how is he?"

"He came to the Gypsy Camp," Melanie said. "Yesterday. He's really worried. He made us promise that if we saw you again, we'd tell you to let him know that you're all right."

"You didn't tell him where I am?"

"How could we? We didn't have a clue where you were. Not after you left without telling anybody like that." Ken was still angry.

"What did he—what did my dad say?"

"Just that he was worried. And he was glad you hadn't been kidnapped," Melanie said.

Toby's eyebrows tilted into a frown. "How did he know that? Oh, I get it. You guys must have told him you'd seen me."

"No, we didn't tell him," April said. "He just kind of guessed."

"Oh yes," Melanie said. "And he told us that you really do have some grandparents who've been trying to adopt you." She smiled ruefully. "We were all really surprised because we thought you were making that up, but he said it was true. But he also said that he wouldn't let them have you. Not ever!"

"Yeah," April put in, "so why'd you have to run away?

Because they couldn't have adopted you if your dad wouldn't let them. I've read about stuff like that, and people who have even one real parent just can't get adopted without that parent's permission. Not even by grandparents."

Toby didn't answer. Instead, he just stared at Melanie and then at April. When he finally spoke, his voice was different, tense and anxious, and even the phony grin was gone. "What else did he say about what they were going to do? About what they were going to do to him if he didn't let me get adopted?"

"What else?" April thought for a moment and then shook her head. "Nothing else about that." She looked at the others. "Do you remember him saying anything about that?"

Nobody did.

"Hey, what could they do?" Ken said.

"I told you, Kamata. Don't you remember? I told you they threatened my dad. And those hit men they brought with them when they came to our apartment? Did you forget about that?"

"No, I didn't forget." Ken's voice was getting tighter all the time. "I just didn't believe you. I mean, what kind of threats did they make? And how did you know about it? Were you there at the time, or did your dad tell you about it afterward?"

Toby's lips twitched. "No, neither one. My dad didn't tell me, and I wasn't there at the time. At least, not officially. See, when my grandparents showed up—the two of them plus these two hired goons—they sent me away. Only

I snuck back and hid in this place I'd fixed up in the brontosaurus, right near where they were sitting."

"In the what?" Ken sounded amazed.

Toby nodded. "Left front leg. I heard everything they said." Suddenly his face seemed to close and darken. "I heard them saying what they were going to do to my dad if he didn't give me up."

Ken got to his feet. "Oh, come on, Tobe. It can't be that bad. I mean who ever heard of killer grandparents?" He was looking around nervously again. "Anyway, we have to get back. So why don't you just grab your stuff and come along."

"Forget it. I'm not coming." Toby's face was tight with anger. "And don't you tell my dad anything. Not anything! I'll do it myself. I'll call him and tell him I'm all right. Okay? So go ahead, leave. Go on. Get out of here."

It was a strangely different Toby Alvillar. April couldn't remember ever seeing Toby really angry before. Cocky and sarcastic and aggravating as hell, sure, but never before just plain old squinty-eyed, shaky-voiced furious.

And Ken was angry, too. "Okay, we will. We'll get out and leave you here to—to—get mugged or—murdered or whatever. Who cares? I sure don't. Come on, everybody. Let's go."

And they did. One by one they went up the stairs and out the door, Ken and April stomping and glaring, Elizabeth crying, and Melanie pulling a whining Marshall behind her. Except for Marshall, nobody even turned to look back.

Twenty-five

HE WAS ALONE again. All that was left was the scuff of footsteps on the stairs and the sound of Elizabeth's sobs— and Marshall's wailing, "Bear. We forgot Bear."

And sure enough, there the big shaggy mutt was, sitting at Toby's feet looking up at him accusingly. Just like the rest of them. Accusing him of being cruel and mean, when he couldn't help what he was doing. When there was absolutely no other way he . . . And then suddenly Ken was dashing back into the basement to grab the belt that was attached to Bear's collar and to pull him toward the door. To drag Bear away without even looking back or saying a word.

It wasn't fair. Didn't Ken know that he wouldn't have run away if there was any other way out of the mess? Didn't he see that? Right at that moment, more than anything in the world he wanted to yell, "Come back. Please come back! Don't leave me here alone."

But he didn't. He couldn't. Instead, just as Ken was almost to the top of the stairs, he yelled, "Hey, Kamata. Look out. You're losing your pants." Ken was grabbing at his pants as he disappeared through the cellar door. Toby tried to laugh.

After he quit trying, he sighed, sat back down on his

blankets with his chin on his fists, and stared into the candle flame. A few moments later he remembered the new bag of food and got up and investigated. Moving the candle closer, he pulled out a bag of cookies, some potato chips, and a huge deli sandwich.

"Great!" he said out loud. "Awesome." He unwrapped the sandwich, stared at it for a moment, and wrapped it back up again. Being angry always did strange things to his stomach, and at the moment it seemed to be turning somersaults. His mind said hungry, but his churning stomach said forget it. He stashed the bag away in the old wooden box where he'd been keeping his backpack when he wasn't using it for a pillow, and sat down again with his chin on his fists. He sat there that way for a long time, thinking. Thinking how unbelievable it was that it had only been four or five days—he wasn't sure just how many— since he'd packed up and snuck out of the studio in the middle of the night. And only about twenty-four hours since he'd heard those strange voices talking to Ken outside the gate of the Gypsy Camp and he had run away again.

The Gypsy Camp. Where the rest of them were going to start playing the new game all about some fairy-tale-type Gypsies who wore bright-colored, bangle-trimmed clothing and gobs of jewelry and who trained animals and told fortunes and danced and sang around their campfires as they kind of commuted around from one gorgeous camping place to another. That was a laugh, he thought, and tried to, but it didn't come out very well. Some game it had turned out to be. Oh, the first part had been a blast all right. The part where February and Company had been really knocked out of their shoes when they found out that he'd been telling the truth about being a Gypsy. Well, at least part Gypsy. But after that it hadn't been much. A few arguments, his dad's crazy painting of a Gypsy caravan, and then—the end. The end for him at least. Probably the rest of them would go on making costumes and trying to train the so-called bear, and learning to tell fortunes, and pretending they were wandering around all over the world, and fighting over what to do next—while he, Toby . . .

Suddenly he was lying on his face on the dirty blankets and, well, not exactly crying but close enough to it to be glad that no one was around to hear the weird noises he was making. After the noises stopped, he went on lying there, thinking and worrying. For a while his mind was mostly on the mess he was in. About what it was like to have no place to live except a pile of dirty blankets in a crummy hideout that really belonged to some weird people who might get tired of having him around at any moment. And nothing to eat, once this new bag was empty. And no friends, now that Ken and the others had given up on him. No people at all except a crazy old beggar woman, a poor retard named Mickey, and skinny Vince, who had killer headaches and a long, sharp knife.

He rolled over, pulling the ragged old blankets higher around his shoulders, and went on thinking about Mickey and Vince. His fellow cellar rats, as Garbo called them. He wondered where they went every day and what they did all day long. Garbo said they'd gone to work, but that couldn't mean real jobs. Not for a lamebrain like Mickey or a guy who could only work in between headache attacks. So that probably meant begging as she did or maybe picking up bottles and other trash to sell the way a lot of poor people

174

had to do. He also thought about how Vince took care of Mickey and how Mickey looked at Vince as if he were some kind of a god.

In between thinking about himself and his fellow cellar rats, Toby spent most of his time thinking about his dad. About how his dad had asked for a message that he was all right, and how on earth he, Toby, could get a message to him without giving everything away. Most of all, without having to explain why he had run away. Because that was the one thing he absolutely couldn't do.

After what seemed like hours of just sitting there worrying, Toby decided to examine his new bag of food again, and this time he did manage to eat the sandwich, a few potato chips, and a cookie or two. After that he got out his flashlight and went to get a drink from the liquor store's water faucet. It was dark and scary outside, and everything was wet and dripping. There had been no sound of rain in the depths of the basement, but obviously there had been quite a lot. He was on his way back to the cellar when he heard mumbling and scuffling feet, and there was Garbo pushing her cart around the corner of the building. A soggy, bad-tempered Garbo, who growled and groaned and smelled like a wet cat.

"You still here," she muttered crossly when she saw Toby. "Dumb kid. Go back where you came from. I don't care how bad it is, kid. It can't be any worse than trying to stay alive in this hell hole."

But a few minutes later, after Toby helped her get her cart down the stairs, she began to warm up a little. "Thanks, kiddo," she said when she was sitting among her blankets and mattresses. "Come back and talk to me in a few minutes after my poor old bones have warmed up a little."

So he went back to his corner and waited, and after a while she called him over and told him to sit down. He did what he was told, but then, when she just sat there staring at him for a long time, he began to think about telling her to forget it and clearing out. Clearing out not just from her corner, but away from the whole disgusting rat hole of a cellar. He probably would have, too, except that right at that moment he was having this desperate feeling that he just had to talk to somebody. Anybody. Even poor old Garbo.

At last Garbo, who had been fussing around with her ragged mittens and wrapping and rewrapping a whole bunch of scarves and shawls around her shoulders, finally looked at Toby and chuckled her sly, sarcastic laugh. "Well, well. Let's see, what was it you said your name was? Not that it matters. You've probably thought of a better one by now. Am I right?"

"My name is really Toby," he surprised himself by saying.

Garbo's sharp glance seemed to pry into his brain. "Really Toby," she said, nodding thoughtfully. "So how do you like being an outcast, Toby, my lad? A throwaway human being?"

Toby decided to try to make it into a joke. "Who's a throwaway human being?" he said, trying to grin. "Not me."

"Yes, you are, dearie." The chuckle was gone now. "Just like everyone else who can't support themselves because they happen to be a little bit different. A little bit too old or

176

too lacking in brainpower or too sick." She flicked her sharp old eyes in Toby's direction. "Or too young." She nodded. "At least in your case, dearie, it's a difference that time may take care of. If you manage to live that long. We throwaway humans tend to die a bit early. Like poor old Jeb, for instance."

"Yeah, I know," Toby said, trying to sound understanding.

Garbo's lips curled in an angry smile. "No, you don't. Not yet, you don't. How could you possibly know anything about the deadly kind of differences that most of us cellar rats have to live with? How could a sharp, young kid like you possibly know anything about it?"

She was glaring at him, and for a minute or two he was speechless, but then suddenly he hit on a good angle. The Gypsy thing. "How could I know anything about being different?" he began. "I'll tell you how. I'll tell you what my whole family and all my ancestors know about being different."

Garbo's glare had faded, and there was interest in her quick glance. "All right, tell me," she said.

So Toby started in on a long story about how he was a Gypsy and how he and all his ancestors had been driven from town to town and country to country because they were "different." He put in a lot that his father had told him about his grandmother's life in Romania, and about the Gypsies in Europe and everything. Putting in all kinds of details that made it sound almost as if he'd been there himself and had seen it all happen. And as he really got into the story, he almost began to believe that he actually had lived in a Gypsy caravan and been chased and persecuted all over everywhere just because he looked different and had different ways of doing things.

Garbo seemed to be buying it. At least she let him go on and on without interrupting, even nodding now and then as if to say she understood. But then, just as he was getting to the most important part, about all the thousands of Gypsies who were killed in the Nazi concentration camps, Garbo suddenly broke in. "All right, enough," she said. "Enough about being a Gypsy. So some of your ancestors were Gypsies. But that was their problem. So how about telling me what *your* problem is? The truth, boy. How about telling me the truth about why you're holed up here with the rest of us cellar rats?"

The truth. There wasn't any good reason to tell anyone the truth right then. Certainly not a crazy old beggar woman. But suddenly the thought of being able to tell someone the whole thing, just as it happened without leaving out any parts or adding any new ones, was kind of like the lifting of a great dark cloud. Taking a deep breath, Toby started at the very beginning.

Twenty-six

APRIL WOULD ALWAYS remember that long walk home after they'd left Toby in the church basement as one of the most awful experiences of her life. Even though she was wide awake and it was still more or less daylight, it had the same feeling as a nightmare. A kind of looming, dark cloud feeling, as if no matter how bad things were at the moment, you knew for certain that they were just about to get a whole lot worse.

The day was fading away, and long spooky shadows were beginning to creep across streets and sidewalks. Marshall was whiny, Elizabeth was sobbing off and on, and Ken was still stomping and glaring. Except to answer Marshall, who kept tugging on them and asking worried questions, nobody tried to make conversation.

The first question Marshall asked was, "Where's Toby?" And when no one answered, he asked it again and again: "Where's Toby? Where's Toby?"

"You know where he is," April said at last. "He's still back there in that cellar."

A little while later Marshall started jerking on the sleeve of Melanie's raincoat. "Does he live there now? Does Toby live in that cellar?"

179

"I guess so," Melanie said. "Stop pulling on me, Marshall. I guess that's where Toby lives now."

"Why?" This time Marshall was tugging on Ken's jacket. "Why does he live there now?"

"How do I know? He didn't tell me anything he didn't tell all of you guys. I guess he just likes it there. I guess the dumb jerk just likes living in a stinking black hole."

Marshall tugged on the jacket again. "But why . . ."

Shoving Marshall's hand away angrily, Ken said, "Cool it with the 'whys.' Okay, kid? I don't have any answers. I don't know *anything* about Toby Alvillar. Not anymore."

After that no one talked. While they were still on Arbor, the only other people they passed were a few ratty-looking characters who all seemed to be in a hurry to get someplace else. And then, wouldn't you know it, just to make matters worse, it began to rain. Not a drenching, soaking kind of rain, but a soggy, miserable drizzle.

Miserable! That was the only word for that whole walk home. But at least nobody laughed at them this time. Not even on Norwich, where there were quite a few other pedestrians. April didn't know exactly why nobody laughed. But for whatever reason the people who glanced up at them from under their umbrellas didn't look like they even wanted to smile.

At the main alley Ken turned off and headed for home, but the rest of them went on to the storage yard. They went back in the way they'd come, through the fence, but after they'd fed Bear and pounded the plank firmly back into place, they went out through the gate, locked it behind them, and went on home. Outside the door of the Rosses' apartment they stopped long enough to remind Marshall again not to say anything about Toby, and then April went on up to the third floor.

At dinner that night, even though April was being careful to act perfectly normal, Caroline seemed to guess that something was wrong. She kept watching with a worried look on her face, and then, when they were just finishing the banana pudding, she came right out and asked.

"April dear," she said, "is anything the matter?"

April looked up quickly and smiled a perfectly normal smile. "The matter?" she said brightly. "Why do you think something's the matter?"

She thought she'd been very convincing, but a few minutes later Caroline asked, "Is it something about Toby? Did you hear something more about Toby this afternoon?"

Fortunately, right at that very moment the phone rang, and it was "the usual" calling for April.

April barely had time to say "Hi" before Melanie said, "Look. Could you come down as soon as you finish eating dinner? My mom says it's okay. I want to talk to you. Privately."

"Yeah," April said, "me too. But what about Marshall?"

Melanie knew what she meant. "Oh, he won't bother us tonight," she said. "My mom's taking care of Jeremy tonight while his folks go to the movies. You know, Jeremy. The kid Marshall always plays with at day care. They're too busy playing cards to bother us."

At least that was what April thought she'd said. "Playing cards?" she said in amazement. Everybody knew that Marshall was pretty sharp for his age, but even smart four-year-olds usually aren't into stuff like bridge or gin rummy.

"Not cards," Melanie said. "Cars! You know, like toy cars and trucks. Anyway, can you come?"

Since it wasn't a school night, Caroline said okay, as soon as April finished putting the dishes in the dishwasher. And Melanie was right about Marshall's not being a nuisance for once. He and his friend were right there pushing things around the living room floor, but they were much too busy to be interested in April's arrival. And once the girls were in Melanie's room, they certainly didn't have to worry about being overheard. Not over the living room's roaring motors and screeching brakes.

"It's gruesome about Toby, isn't it," Melanie said, as soon as the door was closed behind them.

April nodded. "You can say that again."

They kicked off their shoes and sat down cross-legged on Melanie's bed. For a moment they just sat there staring and thinking, and then, at the very same instant, they both shivered and said, "Gruesome!"

It felt good. With all the rotten stuff about Toby to worry about, it was great to have something to feel good about. Something like being mind-reading-type friends again. Melanie's weak grin said as much. They both sighed deeply then and began to talk about Toby.

"Nothing," April said. "I mean, what in the world could we possibly do? We can't go back to that crummy place again, and what could we do if we did? We couldn't make him leave if he doesn't want to."

Melanie nodded. "I know. We absolutely can't go back there. It would be too dangerous. And even if we did go back in a few days"—she paused—"in a few days he might not be there anymore."

"What do you mean, he wouldn't be there? Where do you think he's going to . . ." But then suddenly she knew what Melanie was thinking. Trying to keep her voice calm, April said, "You mean you think he might be dead by then?"

Melanie only nodded and blinked. Her big eyes looked liquid, as if she wasn't far from crying. She swallowed hard before she said, "April, I think we've got to tell someone." When April frowned and shook her head, Melanie went on quickly, with her voice getting higher and shakier, "I know what you think about finking. And I do, too. But it's just that even finking can't be as bad as letting somebody starve to death or catch a terrible disease or maybe even get murdered."

April shook her head stubbornly. "But we promised. We all did. We promised Toby we wouldn't tell anyone."

"I know, I know, but I've been thinking and thinking about Toby, and what I've decided is . . ."

"Yes? What have you decided?" April's chin was jutting and her eyes were narrow.

Melanie gulped and went on, "I've decided that when all the choices are terrible, you have to choose the one that's not as terrible as the other ones. And nothing could be as bad as not to do anything and then find out that Toby . . ." She paused. "It's like my mom says about people who know something terrible is happening, but they don't do anything about it. My mom says people like that have bloody hands."

April went on shaking her head.

But Melanie was determined to finish what she had to say. "And besides, what if Toby made us promise because he's thinking something that isn't true? Like, maybe he thinks his grandparents are going to hire hit men to get his dad if he doesn't give Toby to them. But it could be that Toby is just exaggerating, like always."

"Yeah, I never did believe that stuff about hit men," April said.

"Or maybe Toby honestly thinks his dad was lying and he's planning to let those people have him. Toby could have heard something that made him think that his dad would do that, when he actually wouldn't." Melanie paused and thought and then went on, "You know, I don't think his dad would do that. It's like, when Toby's dad was there in the storage yard that time, I just got this strong feeling that he was really, really worried about Toby. Didn't you?"

April's head shaking had stopped, but she wasn't nodding in agreement either. All she remembered thinking about Andre Alvillar was that he was pretty weird. On the other hand, however, she could see how Toby might have misunderstood what his father was going to do. In her experience, kids and grown-ups went around misunderstanding each other most of the time.

"Okay," April said. "Okay. But I don't see how we could help straighten things out between them. Do you?"

"Well, that's just what I've been thinking about. I've been thinking that maybe we could talk to him. To Toby's father. And kind of make up our own minds about him. About whether he thinks Toby's grandparents have hit men, and if he's actually planning to give Toby up."

"You mean call him on the phone?"

Melanie nodded. "Maybe. Or—"

April interrupted. "That wouldn't do any good. It's too

easy to pretend on the phone. You know, when the other person can't see your face, it's easy to say anything."

"Well, then, maybe we could go see him. Tomorrow's Saturday. And in the morning we could call him up and just ask if we could come over and talk to him."

"No, that's no good. If he knows we're coming, he'll be all ready for us. I mean he'll have some big story ready to tell us." April thought for a second before she went on, "I think it would be better just to call up to see if he's at home, and then if he answers, we'll know he's home and we can—"

"Right. And if he answers, we could just ask him if he's heard anything more about Toby. And not say anything about coming to see him. And then we could hurry over and . . ."

Melanie paused and after a moment they both said, "Yeah," in unison again.

Twenty-seven

BY THE TIME April went back upstairs, they had it all planned. In the morning they would call Andre Alvillar first, to see if he was home. And then they would call Ken to see if he could go, too. Not that April really thought it would do any good. "He won't go," she said. "He's too mad at Toby. He probably wouldn't do anything at all to help Toby now."

So the plan probably wouldn't include Ken. And it definitely wouldn't include Marshall or Elizabeth, because even in the best of circumstances the Alvillar studio wasn't a great place to take little kids. And tomorrow there would be more important things to do than keeping an eye on Marshall and trying to calm down Elizabeth if something scared her. Tomorrow all their attention would have to be on watching Andre Alvillar and trying to decide whether to tell him that Toby was all right. Or where Toby was. Or, maybe, not anything at all.

In bed that night, as she waited to go to sleep, April kept picturing what it would be like tomorrow at the studio and imagining all the things that could go wrong. In her imaginings scary things kept happening, like the huge metal-covered door clanging shut behind them and locking itself so that they couldn't get out. And nobody answering when they called and called and then a strange hairy creature with fiery eyes jumping out at them as they tried to find their way across the enormous cluttered attic.

Then, after she finally went to sleep, the imagined images began to turn into dream scenarios even more incredibly frightening. Scenes in which she and Melanie were chained to the wall in a kind of dungeon, and a strange hairy man kept yelling at them and threatening them with a whip. He was right in the middle of yelling about how they were going to be punished for having bloody hands when April woke up with a start and sat straight up in bed with her heart pounding. It was still dark, so she turned on the light to check the clock. To her surprise it was only a little after four o'clock so after a few minutes she turned the light off. But not before she'd inspected her hands very carefully.

"They're not bloody," she whispered into the darkness, and tried not to imagine a voice answering, "Not yet."

The next morning April and Melanie called the Alvillars' number from the kitchen phone in April's apartment. Caroline had gone out shopping, so they had the apartment to themselves. Since it had been her idea, Melanie did the calling, and afterward April had to admit that she had done a good job. She'd found out that Andre Alvillar was home, but she hadn't said anything about coming to see him.

"What did he say?" April wanted to know as soon as Melanie hung up the phone. "How did he sound?"

"He just said he hadn't heard anything more. And he wanted to know if I had."

"Did he sound strange? You know, nervous or guilty or anything."

Melanie thought for a moment and then nodded. "He

sounded strange all right. Maybe like he was really worried. Or guilty. I guess it could be guilty."

April nodded knowingly and picked up the phone. She wanted to be the one to make the next call, even though she knew it wouldn't do any good. And sure enough, Ken's response was just what she had said it would be.

"You're going to what?" he raved. "You can't do that. We promised. We promised we wouldn't—"

"Wait a minute, wait a minute," April was saying, but when Ken went right on raving, she yelled, *"Will you shut up for a minute and listen!"*

April just went on yelling, drowning Ken out, until he finally ran down long enough for her to get a word in edgewise.

"What I'm trying to tell you is we're not going there to tell him where Toby is. We may not tell him anything. We just want to see if we can figure out why Toby won't go home. And then—"

"Huh," Ken interrupted. "Good luck. I mean, good luck figuring out why Toby Alvillar does anything anymore. What I think is, the dude has just plain gone crazy."

April was yelling again, telling Ken she didn't care what he thought and how he could just forget it, when Melanie took the phone away from her and said, "Ken. Ken, this is Melanie now. Could you just listen for a minute? I want to tell you why we decided we had to go see Toby's father."

Then she went on telling Ken all the things that might happen to Toby if he stayed in that horrible place any longer and why she and April thought he might have run away because of some misunderstanding.

"So we just want to talk to his dad now and, you know, try to decide what we ought to do. And we thought maybe you could help us decide."

Silence. A long, nervous-making silence, before Ken said, "Oh, just talk to him, huh? And then decide? Is that all?" Another long pause, and he went on, "When? When are you going to Toby's place?"

"Pretty soon, I guess. We already asked our folks if we could go to that new game store this morning. You know, Tommy Toy's Toys and Games? And that's not far from where Toby lives, so we thought we'd just—"

"Okay, I get it," Ken interrupted. "Okay. If I decide to come, I'll meet you there, at the game store. In about half an hour. Okay?" But before Melanie could answer, he added, "Maybe I'll be there and maybe I won't." Then the phone went dead.

When April and Melanie started out for Tommy Toy's on the way to Andre Alvillar's studio, they didn't really know whether Ken would show up or not.

"I hope he does," Melanie said as they started down Orchard Avenue. "I'd feel better if there were three of us."

April surprised herself by saying, "Me too." It wasn't every day that she'd choose to have a cocky, know-it-all sixth-grade boy along on any kind of project, but somehow today was different. What made it different was remembering a lot of scary stuff, like how strange Toby's father had been that day when they were all in the studio, as well as remembering the humongous dirty attic itself, with its statues that looked like piles of junk, and piles of junk so high they almost looked like statues. And how the whole place made you feel as if you'd stumbled into some kind of weird alien world. Yes, she had to admit, this was one time she really was hoping for Ken Kamata's company.

But when they got to the game shop, Ken wasn't there. They waited as long as they dared, walking up and down the aisles watching some little kids trying to decide how to spend their Christmas money and then, after they'd hung around for a long time without buying anything, watching how one of the clerks had started eyeing them suspiciously.

Finally, when the clerk came over for the third time to ask if she could help them, Melanie said, "No, thank you. Actually, we're just waiting for a friend, but we're leaving now." She nudged April with her elbow. "Aren't we, April?"

"Yeah, waiting for a friend," April agreed. "But I guess he's not coming, so we might as well go."

They left Tommy Toy's then and went on, walking slowly up University Avenue, stopping to look in windows and to look back over their shoulders to see if Ken might still show up. But they were mainly walking slowly, April knew, simply to put off arriving at the studio as long as possible. At least she knew that was her reason, and she suspected it was Melanie's, too.

But at last there it was, the crummy old building with the bar and pool hall downstairs and, running along beside it, the narrow cluttered alley. And then, halfway down the alley, the rusty iron staircase that led up to the second floor.

At the foot of the stairs they stopped and looked at each

other, a look that silently asked if this was really what they were going to do.

"Well, now that we've come this far, I guess we better go on up. Huh?" April said, making it into a question, just in case Melanie wanted to help change their minds.

But Melanie only sighed and nodded.

Twenty-eight

THE METAL STAIRS creaked with every step, and so did the long platform that led to the entrance of the attic studio. With every rusty shriek April expected to see the heavy door fly open and something terrifying leap out. An angry Andre Alvillar perhaps, shouting and waving his arms. Or maybe, if Toby had been telling the truth, the grandparents' hit men, sinister-looking characters in long overcoats with turned-up collars. As she reached the end of the platform, she was picturing the hit men so vividly that when no one appeared, she went on staring in a kind of disbelief at the solid, rust-streaked surface of the oversized metal door. She was still standing there, frozen with apprehension, when Melanie said, "Where's the doorbell? I don't see a doorbell anywhere."

April swallowed, blinked, and came back to reality. "I guess we'll have to knock," she said.

So they did, softly at first and then more loudly, but there was no answer.

As the minutes passed, April began to feel better. More like her normal, fairly fearless self. "Maybe he went out right after we called," she said, trying not to sound too relieved.

"Maybe," Melanie said. "But maybe he just didn't hear

the knocking. You know how big it is in there. If he's down at the other end of the studio, he might not have heard."

April agreed. "Yeah, you're right. Maybe we could try pounding with . . ." She looked around for something useful, but the metal platform was bare and empty. "Or else we could try kicking. You know, like Toby did." She backed up a few steps, ran forward, and kicked, and the big metal door swung open with a sharp metallic shriek.

They stared at each other in dismay. "I didn't mean to kick it open," April whispered. "I just wanted to make a noise."

Melanie nodded. "I know. He must have heard that if he's home." They waited, peering into the immense expanse of the studio, which, from the doorway, seemed much the same as when they had been there before. Melanie began to move forward, and April followed, winding their way among looming pyramids of artistically arranged trash and around other slightly less artistic-looking piles of junk still waiting to be made into works of art. Overhead a bug-eyed gargoyle face made from egg cartons and camera parts stared down at them, and at shoulder level a shiny clawlike hand reached out to point in their direction. And farther away a long curved neck with tuna-can vertebrae towered up above everything else. The blue brontosaurus.

"He must not be home," Melanie was whispering. "Come on, let's go."

But now April hung back. "Okay," she said, "in a minute. But first I want to look at the brontosaurus. I want to see if Toby could have been telling the truth about hiding in the brontosaurus. You know, when he heard . . ."

Melanie finished the sentence. ". . . what the grand-parents said they would do to his father." She nodded. "Okay. Let's look at the brontosaurus. But hurry. And be very quiet." They tiptoed forward then, choosing their path by keeping the arching neck and tiny head in sight, and a minute or two later there they were, standing beneath the enormous blue body and between the barrel-shaped legs.

In the front leg, Toby had said, but the legs seemed to be completely covered by a stiff blue hide of spray-painted canvas. However, as April ran her hand over the rough surface her fingernails found a loose flap, and when she scratched a little and then pulled—there it was. A perfect hiding place inside the metal framework and wrinkled hide of the left front leg.

She even tried it out to be sure it was possible, slipping easily into the large hollow space and closing the canvas flap behind her. It was very dark inside. The thick blue hide shut out all the light except for a narrow beam that came from what seemed to be a slit in the canvas. A slit through which you could peer out at—something new. Something she was sure she hadn't seen before. Scrambling out, she pulled Melanie around the enormous legs to where they both could see. "Look," she almost yelled, entirely forget-ting to keep her voice down. "Look what's right out there."

The something new was a kind of living room area: two old leathery couches, a couple of chairs, and even a coffee table made from half an old oil drum. A sitting area that certainly hadn't been there a little over a week ago when they had wandered around the brontosaurus looking for the way out. But now there it was. A place where visitors might be invited to sit down to chat—or, if they happened to be evil grandparents or hired goons, to threaten to do terrible things to anyone who wouldn't give in to their demands.

April and Melanie stared at each other in amazement. "He could have," April whispered, and Melanie nodded.

"So maybe he was telling the truth after all," she said.

They were still standing there staring back at Toby's hiding place when there was a faint scuffling noise that came from someplace very near, and a deep voice said, "Who? Who was telling the truth after all?" And when they whirled around, he was standing right behind them.

Andre Alvillar's long curly hair was a stringy mop around his bearded face, and his dark Gypsy eyes looked sunken and shadowed. As the two girls stared in silent shock, he repeated the question. Looking directly at Melanie and then at April, he asked, "Who could have been telling the truth?" And when they only shook their heads, he changed the question to, "Was it Toby? Was it Toby who could have been telling the truth?"

April felt her head twitch from an almost nod to an almost shake and back again, and she was just opening her mouth to say something or other, when there was a loud series of noises that seemed to be coming from the other end of the studio. The noises grew louder and went from clang to clump and then to a prolonged clatter as if someone had tripped over a pile of trash. And a moment later someone dashed around the rear end of the brontosaurus and slid to a stop. It was Ken Kamata, looking as if he'd just finished running a long-distance race. His whole face was red and sweaty, his mouth was hanging open, and he looked absolutely awful. April had never been so glad to see anyone in her whole life.

"Where have you been?" she said angrily. "You promised to meet us at Tommy Toy's."

Ken glared back. "I tried," he gasped. "I got hung up. My mom made me clean up my room. I came as fast as I could—"

"Ken," Andre Alvillar broke in. "Now that you're here, I'll ask you the same question. I just overheard the girls here saying 'someone might have been telling the truth after all,' but they seem reluctant to explain. What I'd like to know is if they were referring to Toby. And if so, where and when he told you this truth." He paused, and when he went on, his voice had a strange quaver. "And also, I'd be everlastingly grateful if you'd tell me if you've had any contact with Toby since I saw you on Thursday."

Ken's face closed down like a slammed door. His lips pressed tightly together as if to keep the slightest hint from escaping, and his narrowed eyes told April and Melanie that they'd better do the same.

No one spoke. Andre Alvillar looked from Ken to April to Melanie and back again. At last he nodded, leaned forward, and seemed to take a deep new breath as if he'd been holding on to the last one for a long time. "All right. All right. You've promised not to tell. But perhaps you haven't promised not to tell me this. If you know, please, *please* tell me why Toby ran away."

Still no one answered. Andre sighed. "Perhaps you'll feel you can answer if I put it this way. Did he think he was going to have to go to live with his grandparents? Did he think I was going to sign the papers?"

Melanie was nodding. She glanced defiantly at April and Ken before she whispered, "Maybe. Maybe that too, but I think it was more because—because he had to protect someone."

"Protect someone? Who?" Andre threw up his hands in a strange, wild gesture. "Why would he think he had to do that?"

All at once April found herself answering. She hadn't intended to at all, but suddenly she was saying, "Because of something he heard when no one knew he was listening. Because of what he heard when you were talking to his grandparents, and he got sent away. Only he didn't really go away."

For a long moment Andre stared at April in what seemed to be amazement or disbelief. "What do you mean he didn't go away? I'm sure he . . . I checked. Where could he have—"

"Right there," April said triumphantly, pointing to the brontosaurus's left leg. "See, like this." Moving forward, she pulled back the loose flap of blue hide.

Andre was staring, open-mouthed, his dark-rimmed eyes blank and unblinking. Like a person in a trance he moved toward the leg, lifted the flap, stared inside, and then carefully replaced it. And when he turned back to face them, there was a difference in his thin hairy face. A mysterious difference. It wasn't exactly anger or fear or joy, although it might have been a little bit of all three. But whatever it was, it changed everything miraculously. The biggest miracle was what it did to Ken.

When Ken, who had been staring at the brontosaurus leg hiding place too, let his eyes move to Andre's face, he suddenly began to babble, spilling out everything he knew, just as if he hadn't been the one who'd always said they couldn't tell anybody anything—not anything—not ever! "Yeah," he suddenly began to jabber, "he told us about that hiding place. He said he hid there and heard everything you guys were saying."

Andre's glowing eyes turned to Ken. "Did he tell you what he heard?" he asked.

"Yeah, he told us. He said he heard you talking to his grandparents and these two hit men they brought along with them, and he heard them say that if you didn't do what they said, they were going to . . ." He drew his finger across his throat.

Andre nodded, and for just a moment his lips, under the curly beard, seemed to curve upward in a smile. "I see," he said. "And did he say who it was that was going to do the . . . ?" He copied Ken's throat-slashing motion.

Ken frowned. "Not exactly. Well, sort of. He sort of said the hit men would do it. He said the grandparents had these two killer types with them."

"Killer types?" Andre's lips twitched again. "Let's see if I have this right. The two hit men who came with Toby's grandparents were going to do me in"—he repeated the neck-slashing motion—"if I didn't give Toby up to them?" His eyes went from Ken to April and then on to Melanie. They all nodded solemnly.

Suddenly Andre began to laugh. He laughed for what seemed an amazingly long time while April and Melanie and Ken stared at him and at one another, not knowing what to say or do. Afterward Melanie told April that she'd never known before that you could tell so much about a person by the way he laughed. April knew what she meant. It was true at least that when Andre Alvillar finally stopped laughing and asked the one question they'd promised each other not to answer, they all began to talk at once.

"He's in the basement of this old church . . . ," April began, while Ken was saying, "On Arbor Street. Way up past . . . ," and Melanie was adding, "He's probably still there. We saw him there yesterday."

"An old church on Arbor Street?" Andre asked as he was pulling on his jacket. "You're certain?"

They were still standing there nodding when Andre ducked under the brontosaurus and the sound of his running footsteps faded away in the distance.

Twenty-nine

IT HAD BEEN the evening before, at almost the same time that April and Melanie were planning their visit to Andre's studio, that Toby started telling Garbo about being a Gypsy. And it was only a little later when he suddenly decided to knock off the tall tales and tell her the real story. Right from the beginning.

"Well, see, the real beginning . . . ," Toby started, and then stopped to eye Garbo suspiciously. "You won't tell anybody? Promise me you won't tell anybody?"

Garbo shrugged. "Who would I tell, dearie? Who do I know who has time to worry about the terrible problems of a smart, healthy kid like you?"

"Yeah, okay." Toby took a deep breath. "See, it's like this. My mother's been dead since I was about five years old. Her name was Joanna Mayfield, and she met my dad when they were both students at the university. They were both studying to be artists, only my father was this poor, kind of weird, Gypsy artist on a scholarship and my mother was—well, she was one of the Mayfields."

He checked to see if Garbo had heard of the Mayfields, but she only shook her head, so he went on. "Anyway, when they got married, the Mayfields hated it a lot. They hated my dad the most, I guess, but they even started hating my mother, who was their own daughter, and when I was born they hated me, too. Or I guess they must have, because they never tried to see me or anything like that. But then, when I was about five years old something really terrible happened and—and—my mother died."

Toby stopped to consider. He'd never, ever told anyone about any of this stuff before. Instead, when kids asked him about his mother, he usually said he'd never had one, like maybe he was just some kind of laboratory product or something. He checked Garbo. She was looking at her fingerless gloves again, but there was something about her face that made him think she'd been listening. Really listening. And for some weird reason Toby really wanted to go on. Wanted to so much that it was as though he just couldn't make himself shut up.

"There was this big party, see. In the studio where we lived back then, which was on the top floor of a big apartment building. And someone who was there brought some dope. Something that you could put in a drink. And either he put it in my mom's drink or else the drinks got mixed up. My dad doesn't know which. Anyway, my mom went up on the roof, and then I guess she fell off. I mean, that must have been what happened. Anyway, there was a big investigation and everything. I was pretty young at the time, so I didn't understand much about what was going on, but I did know everything was different after that."

"Different?" It was the first question Garbo had asked.

"Well, yeah. There were just the two of us after that. And we moved a couple of times. And my dad changed a lot. Things were pretty gross for a while, but then my dad started to get a little better and I started going to a different school and everything was okay. Not great sometimes, but okay. But then, just a few months ago, the Mayfields showed up again and wanted to adopt me. Which was really weird because I was already eleven years old, and up until then they'd never even sent me a lousy birthday card."

Garbo nodded. "So why? Must be a reason."

"Right. There is. See, the Mayfields apparently have this thing about having grandchildren to carry on the name and like that. But for a long time they didn't think they needed me because my mother had a younger brother. This guy named Warren Mayfield the Third. I guess they were kind of counting on him to get married and come up with lots of little Mayfields. But then, just lately I guess, they found out that he's not going to have any kids, so I was the next best thing. So they decided to let me be Warren Mayfield the Fourth. But only if they could adopt me and change my name and everything. So anyway, my dad said it was up to me. He even let me go to visit them one weekend to see if I liked it."

"And . . . ?"

"I *hated* it. I mean, it was the pits. They live in this huge, old, boring house way out in the country. Like a museum full of all kinds of fancy stuff that you don't dare touch unless you've just washed your hands. And most of it, not even then. And I had to practically ask permission to breathe, and I had to call them Grand-moth-er May-field and Grand-fath-er May-field, and—and . . . I hated it. Boy, did I hate it."

"So your dad said . . ."

"He told them no. But then, right after Christmas, he got a letter from a lawyer who said that he and the

202

Mayfields and some kind of a caseworker were going to come to see us. Like, whether we wanted them to or not. The letter didn't say why they were coming, but my dad said they were probably going to see if they could prove that I was living in an unhealthy environment or something like that, so the state could legally take me away."

"An unhealthy environment. Dear me, how dreadful," Garbo said, looking around at the dark, dirty basement. Toby saw what she meant.

"Yeah," he said. "Well, the thing is, we, my dad and I, live in this big old studio on top of a bar and pool hall, and it's not exactly *Good Housekeeping*, if you know what I mean. So we decided we'd better straighten things up a little before they got there. So we got started on it. My dad fixed up the kitchen, and one of my dad's friends, my dad has a lot of great friends, gave us these neat old leather couches. So we fixed up a new living room area. And we were going to get everything all cleaned up, only they showed up early. Like three days before they said they were coming and . . ."

Toby couldn't help grinning a little, remembering how all four of them had walked in on the afternoon of New Year's Eve. His dad had left the outside door open to air the place out a little, and suddenly there they were.

"And then suddenly there they were," he told Garbo. "Old Mayfield"—Toby jumped up and did a dignified overstuffed waddle—"in a suit and overcoat, and Grandmother Mayfield in this big mink coat."

"A mink coat?" Garbo asked, making her eyebrows say how impressed she was.

"Yeah. You couldn't prove it by me, but my dad said it

was probably mink." He grinned. "He also said it was Grandma's personality that made it seem more like grizzly bear."

Garbo chuckled appreciatively as Toby sat down and went on: "And they had these other dudes with them who were . . ." He paused and grinned ruefully, remembering what he'd told the other kids about the two hit men.

"Who were . . . ," Garbo prompted him.

"Well, there was just the one man, really. The lawyer was this tall guy with a real phony smile. The caseworker was short and blond and—well, actually she's a woman. But anyway, all four of them walked in just when my dad and I were goofing off a little." Toby grinned again, remembering. "Well, we were having a duel actually, with a mop and broom and garbage can lids for shields. My dad's really good at fencing, so I kept getting mortally wounded, and I was right in the middle of this dramatic death scene—I do a great death scene—when we looked up, and there they were. Standing around in a circle staring down at me." Toby might have laughed out loud, if it hadn't been for what happened next.

"So, what happened next?" Garbo asked, as if she could read his mind.

"So, next . . ." Toby took a deep breath. "The lawyer said they had to talk to my dad in private, so I got sent away. Only I snuck back into this great hiding place I'd fixed up and heard everything they said."

"And they said . . . ?"

Toby's face began to feel tight and hot. He had to work at unclenching his jaw before he could say, "That they had reason to believe that my dad was a drug user and that if he didn't agree to the adoption, there would be an investigation." He swallowed hard and tried to control the screech that was building up in his voice. "Which is a big lie. My dad doesn't use drugs. Not at all. Maybe he did a long time ago. I don't know about that. But he sure doesn't now. Not since—well, you know."

Garbo nodded. "Yes, I see."

"But the worst part was that this lawyer dude said they'd probably have to reopen the investigation about what happened to my mother. They'd bring all that up again—and . . ." For a minute Toby couldn't go on. "He couldn't take it," he finally managed to say. "I just know he couldn't take it again." Covering his face with his hands, he sat for a long time without saying anything. Garbo didn't say anything either. When he was sure he could talk normally again, he took his hands away and said, "After they left, my dad told me everything was all right. He didn't know I'd been listening. But I could tell everything *wasn't* all right. Not anywhere near all right. My dad looked . . . Well, I can remember how he used to look right after my mom died. I was pretty little, but I'll never forget that. I'll never forget how I used to think he was going to die too. That he was going to die on purpose so he wouldn't have to go on feeling the way he was feeling. It used to scare the hell out of me. And now he'd started looking that way again. So then, that night after we'd gone to bed I began to think about how, if I was out of the picture, the Mayfields wouldn't have any reason to bother him anymore, and maybe they'd forget about bringing up all that stuff about my mother, and then my dad would be . . ."

It was just about then, while Toby was right in the middle of explaining why he'd had to run away, when he became aware that someone else was in the basement. Someone besides himself and Garbo. And when he whirled around, there they were, a soggy Vince and Mickey, standing just inside the door, dripping rainwater into a big puddle at their feet. Like, maybe they'd been there for a long time, quietly dripping and listening to everything he'd said. Toby got to his feet, nodded coolly to the two wet cellar rats, and went back to his own corner. It wasn't until he was under the blankets that he really began to lose it.

He stayed there under the covers for maybe half an hour. Maybe longer. Now and then he could hear voices: Mickey's squeaky and high-pitched one and Vince's deep, slurred rumble. But he couldn't hear what they were saying. No one tried to bother him while he was under the blankets, but when he finally did come out, he was surprised to find Mickey squatting just a few feet away, holding something in his hands and smiling his gargoyle grin.

"Hi," Mickey said. "For you. Vince got them for you." He was holding out a little packet of soda crackers. Just two crackers in a plastic wrapper, the kind you get in restaurants to eat with your soup.

"Thanks. Thanks a lot." Toby took the crackers and tore open the top of the package. Across the room candles were burning in the corner where Vince was writing in a notebook. In her alcove, Garbo seemed to be asleep. Toby ate the crackers slowly, while Mickey went on staring and grinning. The dry, crumbly crackers went down hard and scratchy around the lump in Toby's throat. When he'd finished eating, he thanked Mickey again and tried to grin back at him, without much luck.

"Mickey," Vince said. "Give it a break. Go to bed."

"Okay. Okay, Vince," Mickey said. Getting clumsily to his feet, he stared down at Toby. When he put out his big, stubby-fingered hand, Toby couldn't help pulling away, but all the poor guy did was pat him on the head. As if he were a dog or something. Then Mickey went off to his pile of blankets and, after a lot of flopping around, got into a beat-up old sleeping bag and went to sleep. Toby went back to bed, too. He was still lying there wide awake when he heard a sound and opened his eyes. It was Vince, standing right there beside his bed. In the flickering light of a candle his dark face was almost invisible.

"Look kid." His voice was so soft Toby had to strain to hear. "Go on home. What can they do to him that would be as bad as not knowing where you are?"

He went away then, back to his corner. The candle went out, and Toby was left in the dark, trying not to think about what Vince had said.

But I'm going to call him tomorrow, he told himself. *That is, I will if I can find a pay telephone. And if I can get enough money for the call. I'll just call, and when he answers, I'll say I'm all right, and then I'll hang up before he has time to ask me where I am.*

He thought about what he would say for a long time. Then he must have slept for a while and dreamed about it. In the dream his dad answered the phone, but all he said was that everything was fine, the way he always did when you asked him what was the matter. What he'd always said, even when things were the worst.

When Toby woke up, he could tell it was already late morning. Saturday morning. He listened for a minute to be sure the other cellar rats were still sleeping, and then he got up and put all his stuff into his backpack. All except for what was left of the bag of cookies, which he left on the floor beside Mickey's sleeping bag. Then he tiptoed to the door, climbed out, and started down Arbor Street on his way to University Avenue and Maple.

It wasn't so much that he'd changed his mind, because he really hadn't. His mind didn't seem to have had anything to do with it. It was as though some other part of him had made the decision. He was still on Arbor Street, walking faster and faster, when he heard someone shout his name, and there was his father, running toward him.

Grabbing him by the shoulders, his dad shook him fiercely, laughing and yelling stuff like, "You crazy kid. You crazy, idiotic, courageous kid!"

Toby grinned back at him and said, "Yeah, I'm glad to see you too."

Thirty

"ALL RIGHT, YOU JERKS," April practically shouted. "Come to order so we can get started, or else get out of here."

What April was trying to get started at that particular moment was the first Gypsy meeting since the return of Toby, which was already almost two weeks ago. The meeting was being held in April's living room, and everybody was there. April and Melanie were sitting on the floor. Elizabeth was curled up in Caroline's recliner chair, and Ken and Toby had taken over the couch, not to mention the coffee table, where Ken was doing something with a deck of cards. Marshall was curled up with Bear in front of the fireplace.

That's right, Bear. And it wasn't the first time he'd been in the Casa Rosada, either. He'd been spending quite a lot of time at the Halls' and the Rosses' ever since the adults found out about him *and* heard how he'd helped to solve the mystery of Toby's disappearance. And then it had turned out that although dogs (or bears) were not permitted as permanent residents in the Casa Rosada, there were no rules against having one as an occasional visitor. So now that Bear, officially speaking, belonged to Toby and lived at the Alvillars', he could make fairly lengthy visits to the Halls or the Rosses without anyone complaining. Especially since he'd been to the vet's for a couple of antiflea treatments. Today just happened to be one of Bear's days to visit April and Caroline, so there he was right in the middle of the big, important meeting to decide the future of the Gypsy Game.

As far as April was concerned, having Bear as an occasional visitor had some good results and some not so good. One of the good surprises was that it turned out that Caroline had always been a dog lover, and she liked having a part-time dog almost as much as April did.

But then there was the Toby thing. Since Toby usually was the one who brought Bear over for his Casa Rosada visits, it meant that he was around quite a bit, too. April wasn't too sure just how she felt about that. A couple of times when he was delivering Bear, he came on in and sat at the kitchen table long enough to have a Pepsi and talk to Caroline for a while.

All kinds of people liked to talk to Caroline. That's what April told Melanie and Elizabeth when they teased her about Toby's visits. Anyway, she told them, they were just jealous because everyone was dying of curiosity to know why Toby had run away and how everything was going now that he was back with his dad. And having Toby around so much meant that April and her grandmother were the first ones to find out things like the kinds of threats the Mayfields actually had made, and how they turned out to be not all that dangerous.

"Yeah," Toby had admitted—to Caroline, of course, "I was kind of exaggerating when I said they were threatening to . . ." He made the throat-cutting motion. But then he went on and told about what the Mayfields had really threatened to do if his dad didn't cooperate. All about the lies they were going to tell about his dad and how they were going to reopen the investigation into Toby's mother's death.

"How awful," Caroline said. "What a cruel thing to do."

Toby nodded, and for a moment there was a strangely serious expression on his face. Then he laughed and said, "But I guess they backed down right away when my dad sicced Roger on them. Roger Wallace the lawyer, that is. See, my dad and Roger have been friends since way back when they were kids, and Roger said the Mayfields didn't have a leg to stand on and that my dad had all kinds of proof that he hadn't had anything to do with what happened to my mother. And that he's been a good father too. Well, not your usual neighborhood Boy Scout leader, Little League coach type, maybe, but not all that bad either." Toby grinned. "Except for the canned tuna, that is. That's what I told Roger. That, except for the canned-tuna diet, my dad never tortured me at all. And then the caseworker turned out to be sort of on our side, and after she and Roger talked to the Mayfields' lawyer they decided to drop the whole adoption thing. And the way it wound up, everybody cooled off some, and I might even visit them once in a while, as long as they let me decide when I want to leave." Then he grinned again and said, "End of story."

End of that story anyway. But there was something else that had to be settled right away. Something April and Melanie had been working on for about a week. And that was what was going to happen to the Gypsy Game now that Toby was back home. The two girls had talked a lot

211

about having a meeting and how they thought the other kids would vote, but the strange thing was they never really discussed what they, themselves, wanted to do. Not since the night that they'd had the big argument when Melanie said she thought having a game about Gypsies just wasn't going to work. April wasn't sure why they hadn't discussed it, unless it was just that they didn't want to risk having another fight. And having the meeting would be a good way to let the other kids do the arguing.

It hadn't been easy to arrange. As a matter of fact it had taken an awful lot of phone calls. Elizabeth agreed to come right away, of course, but Ken and Toby weren't all that enthusiastic.

"What's the rush?" Ken said the first time they called him. "Nobody's going to be doing anything in that muddy old storage yard until the rain stops. Besides, I couldn't be there very often. Not for a while anyway. I just signed up for after-school basketball."

Toby seemed a little more interested. "Oh yeah," he said. "You mean that game where I was going to get to be the VIP king of the Gypsies and tell everybody what to do?" But even after April set him straight on that one, he still said he might show up if they had a meeting.

But after everyone finally arrived on a rainy Saturday morning and goofed around a lot and ate up all the cookies, Ken and Toby kept on wasting time with a deck of trick playing cards that Ken had brought to the meeting. Even after April got out her notebook and got ready to take notes, Ken and Toby just went on with what they were doing. Even after she asked them nicely to knock it off two or three times, and finally not so nicely. Like yelling, "All right, you jerks. Come to order so we can get started, or else get out of here."

"*Sheesh*. Listen to old February," Ken said. "Who elected you president?"

April gave him one of her icy stares. "Nobody did. But whose house is this, and whose grandmother made the cookies? And besides, I thought we were here on important business."

Ken went on shuffling. "Like what?"

"You know like what. I told you on the phone. I told you that—"

"Yeah, I know," Ken interrupted, "but what's the hurry? Like I said, we're not going to be able to do anything out there for a long time. It'll be too cold and muddy—"

"We know that," Melanie broke in. "But we, I mean I, think that maybe we need to decide whether or not to go on with the Gypsy Game. Because if we are going to, we could do a bunch of stuff at home right now, like making costumes and collecting stuff and"—she looked at April—"and reading books. You know, about Gypsies, like we did about Egypt, even when we couldn't go outside. And if we're *not* . . ."

That seemed to get Ken's attention, at last, and Toby's too. "What do you mean if we're not?" Toby asked. He stared at Melanie and then at April. "Oh, I get it," he said, doing one of his most aggravating grins. "Like, no more playing games where a certain person isn't the *natural-born* leader. Let's see. You look kind of Irish, February. What are we going to do next? The Irish Game?"

April had to work at it, but she managed to stay cool.

"As a matter of fact," she said in an icy tone of voice, "I'm not the one who wanted to stop. Am I, Melanie? Tell them about it, Melanie. Okay? Tell them why you didn't want to do the Gypsy thing anymore."

Melanie looked embarrassed. "I didn't say for sure I didn't want to. I only said that finding out all those horrible things that happened to Gypsies was too . . . well, it was too depressing, I guess."

"Oh yeah? Horrible?" Ken finally looked interested. "What kind of horrible things?"

So Melanie began to tell about the things she'd read in *The Eternal Outcasts*. All about how Gypsies had been beaten and killed and sold into slavery, all over the world, for hundreds and hundreds of years. And then how Hitler and the Nazis had killed so many thousands more.

By the time Melanie finished, Elizabeth's eyes were full of tears, which was pretty much what you'd expect of a sensitive fourth grader. But Ken was more of a surprise. He'd quit kidding around, and the questions he asked were pretty serious. Toby's reaction had changed too.

"Yeah," he said when Melanie finally ran down, "I know all that stuff. My dad told me a long time ago. I just didn't think you guys would be interested."

"What do you mean, you didn't think we'd be interested?" April asked. "Don't you think we want to know the truth about things, even if some of it is too horrible to play games about? What I think is . . ." Noticing the surprised look on Melanie's face, April lost her train of thought, but after a moment she went on. "What I think is—it's just too depressing."

After that it got quiet and stayed that way for an incredibly long time. As if nobody could come to a decision or even think of anything to say. For several minutes the only sound was the rain spattering against the windows and a soft snoring noise from across the room, where both Marshall and Bear were sound asleep.

Toby spoke first, but what he started discussing wasn't *The Eternal Outcasts* or the Gypsy Game or even real Gypsies. What Toby started telling was about Garbo and Vince and Mickey.

Of course they'd all heard about the three of them before, the old beggar lady and the two guys who'd been living in the church basement. Toby had told how his three temporary roommates hadn't tried to rob or hurt him or anything, and how Vince, actually, had been the one who'd persuaded him to go back to his father. But this time Toby told them quite a lot more.

This time he told them more about Vince's headaches, which made him almost blind and crazy with pain, and how Mickey was like a huge overgrown two-year-old. And that Garbo had told him that both Mickey and Vince had been in hospitals for a while until there wasn't any money for them anymore, and they got sent out to learn to be responsible and self-sufficient.

And how Garbo, herself, had no place to live because she didn't have any family and was too much of an oddball to fit into the kinds of institutions they wanted to put her in. And so she'd been on the streets for a long time, begging for money for food and living wherever she could.

"Garbo told me all sorts of stuff about them and what it was like to be what she called throwaway human beings," Toby said. "That's what she called them. All three of them,

215

and me too while I was there." Toby's grin was one-sided and brief. "And cellar rats. She called us cellar rats. And outcasts, too." He looked at Melanie. "Just like in that book you were talking about."

"Outcasts," Toby said. And then he was quiet again for a while before he sighed and grinned in a strange way and said, "It's not a whole lot of fun, being an outcast. Eternal or otherwise."

There was another long quiet spell before Ken said, "Hey, I got it. How about if we kind of try to help those dudes out a little? I mean, Garbo and those other dudes." He looked around the group and then nodded. "You know, like getting some kind of project started for—"

"Hold it. Hold everything, Kamata," Toby said. "My dad already thought of that. He's already been over to see Garbo a bunch of times. And he's been talking to some of his friends about finding a place for people like them to live and—"

Ken interrupted back, "Hey, I'll bet my dad could help with that kind of real estate thing. I'll ask him. I'll ask my dad."

Then they all started having ideas, about bake sales and car washes and other ways to raise money. April was just saying that Melanie ought to be treasurer because she was good at math and keeping track of money, when Marshall woke up.

Getting up from where he'd been lying with his head on Bear's neck, he wobbled over sleepily, rubbing his eyes. "Hi," he said. "What are we talking about?" He looked at Melanie. "Are we talking about the Gypsy Game?"

216

Melanie started to say, "No. Not about the—" when April interrupted.

"That's right," she said. "A game about a different kind of Gypsies. I guess we're talking about a different kind of Gypsy Game."

Marshall looked worried. "With bears?" he asked anxiously.

"Sure, Marshamosis," Toby said. "With bears. Couldn't have a Gypsy Game without a bear, could we?"

Everybody laughed and went back to making plans about ways to raise money, and maybe for another type of meeting to which parents and other adults might be invited.

Everybody seemed pretty enthusiastic, at least for the moment. But later, when Ken and Toby and Elizabeth had gone home and Marshall had gone back to playing with Bear, April and Melanie talked about some of the problems that might arise and how much harder it would be this time because of having to get adults to agree on what ought to be done and how to do it and especially on who was going to get to run things and make all the important decisions.

"There's going to be a lot of arguments," April said. "Adults have a hard time agreeing on who gets to run things."

"I know." Melanie was looking worried. "It's definitely not going to be easy. There's going to be a lot of . . ."

"A lot of what?"

"Well, you know. Ethical dilemmas, and stuff like that."

"Yeah." April sighed. But then she grinned and said. "But we can handle it, I guess. I mean, we're practically experts at ethical dilemmas. Right?"

"Right!" Melanie grinned back. "Practically experts."

About the Author

ZILPHA KEATLEY SNYDER has written many distinguished and popular books for children, including *The Egypt Game, The Headless Cupid,* and *The Witches of Worm,* all Newbery Honor Books and American Library Association Notable Books for Children. Her most recent books for Delacorte Press are *The Trespassers* and *Cat Running,* a *School Library Journal* Best Book of the Year.

Zilpha Keatley Snyder lives in Marin County, California.

Turn the page for a preview of life
in turn-of-the-century America in *Gib Rides Home* . . .

BY THE AUTHOR OF *THE EGYPT GAME*

GIB RIDES HOME

Zilpha Keatley Snyder

On sale now wherever books are sold.

Delacorte Press

0-385-32267-4

CHAPTER

1

On a dark, cloudy afternoon in the fall of 1909, a strange thing happened on the third floor of the Lovell House Home for Orphaned and Abandoned Boys. Something so downright mysterious that even firsthand witnesses could scarcely believe their eyes. What those witnesses, five amazed and startled senior boys, saw that dull, gray afternoon was the sudden and entirely unexpected reappearance of a boy who had left the orphanage more than a year before.

No one had heard from Gibson Whittaker since he went away, but the rumor was that he had been adopted by a family who lived near Longford, a small cattle town in the next county. There was nothing especially uncommon about that. Half, or even full, orphans left Lovell House fairly often, going back with a remaining parent or out to an adoption, but what was so shocking was his reappearance. How could Gib Whittaker be strolling into the senior boys' dormitory when the law said, at least the law according to Miss Offenbacher, that Lovell House adoptions were not reversible? In other words, when you left the orphanage you left it for good and always.

The sun had already gone down when Gib arrived, and the third-floor Senior Hall was dimly lit. The supper bell was due to ring soon and the long hall, with its orderly rows of narrow beds, was almost deserted. Of the sixteen boys who were seniors that year, only five were in the room and they were running late. Since they'd spent their afternoon chore time mucking out stalls in the orphanage's barn and cowshed, more than the usual amount of changing and scrubbing had been necessary.

Being late for supper was dangerous, but so was arriving at the table in an unsanitary condition, so the situation was serious, but not quite serious enough to prevent a certain amount of fooling around. Some shoving and splashing was going on as the five boys crowded around the washbasin nearest the hall door. The water in the basin was cold, and gasps and giggles were echoing through the high-ceilinged room, when the shriek of door hinges caused a sudden silence. As one, the gigglers hushed, froze, and then turned anxiously, expecting Mr. Harding, maybe, or even Miss Offenbacher. But instead, there he was, Gibby Whittaker.

For a second, no more than a split second probably, nobody recognized him, not even Jacob Fetters and

Bobby Whitestone. And Jacob and Bobby had known Gib since back when they'd been little old juniors together.

But under the circumstances, Bobby and Jacob's blank stares weren't too surprising. After all, Gib had been ten years old when he went away and now he had to be almost twelve. He'd filled out a little, gotten some taller, and no longer had the typical Lovell House haircut—a near scalping by a local barber whose "orphans' special" was quick and cheap, if not particularly good to look at.

He was dressed differently, too. Instead of the scratchy wool suit of institutional navy blue, he was wearing a fringed leather jacket over mud-stained denim pants. And on his feet, instead of the standard orphanage clodhoppers, were a pair of boots. Scuffed and dusty boots, certainly, but with a style about them that had nothing to do with living in an orphanage, or for that matter anywhere else in downtown Harristown.

So the hair and clothes were different all right, but there were some things about Gib Whittaker that weren't ever likely to change. He was still lanky and tall for his age, with a slow and easy way about him, and a grin that did something to his eyes before it began to stretch first one side of his wide mouth and then the other.

So it was Gib sure enough, right back there in the third-floor dormitory where nobody had ever expected to see him again. But what made his reappearance even more amazing was what he'd brought with him. What Gib Whittaker was toting into the seniors' dormitory along with an ordinary old duffel bag, was what appeared to be an honest-to-God saddle. An honest-to-goodness old roping saddle.

"Gibby," somebody finally yelped, Jacob or Bobby probably. Gib grinned, and then, while the others stared like a bunch of dummies, he sauntered down the hall, dumped the bag and saddle on the floor beside bed number five, shoved them under with one foot, stuck his hands in his pockets, and nodded, first at straw-headed old Jacob and then at skinny-as-ever Bobby Whitestone.

"Jacob," he said, and then, "How you been, Bobby?"

A new boy, someone Gib had never seen before, was poking Jacob and whispering, "Who—who—who," like he'd been turned into some kind of big-eared, towheaded owl.

"Stop that, Jackie." Jacob elbowed the new kid out of his way. "Don't you know nothing? It's Gib. Gib Whittaker." But Jackie, who wasn't especially quick-witted, went on staring blank-eyed. It wasn't until Bobby Whitestone spoke up that Jackie and the other new boys began to understand. "You know," Bobby said, "the Gib we told you about, who got adopted a long time ago."

Jackie's "Ohh! That Gib," was long and drawn out as a sigh. They'd all heard about that Gib Whittaker.

Knobby-headed little Bobby Whitestone, who had been at Lovell House ever since Infant Room, was looking as walleyed as a wild mustang. Bobby had always been a worrier. And a whiner. His voice had a high-pitched wobble to it as he asked, "What happened, Gib? How come you're back?"

Bobby had good reason to be worried about Gib and about what might happen to him now. Everybody knew how dangerous it was to run out on an adoption. Especially to run out on certain kinds of adoptions.

Jacob Fetters, who, like Bobby, had been in Junior Hall with Gib, looked worried too, his blotchy face scrunched up into a twitchy grimace. "Where you been, Gib?" he asked. "Miss Mooney said you'd been sure enough adopted by some people near Longford. Some real rich folk, name of . . ." Jacob looked around, asking someone to help him remember. "Name of . . . ?"

It was Gib himself who answered. "Name of Thornton," he said solemnly. Then he grinned at Jacob and added, "The Thorntons live pretty near Longford all right, and I guess they're fair-to-middling rich. Miss Mooney got that part just about right."

Jacob nodded, and his sympathetic shrug said he could guess what Miss Mooney had been wrong about—the kind of adoption it was.

"Yes sir," Gib went on, his halfway grin hinting that there was something more to what he was saying than just the words, "I been with the banking Thornton family for almost—"

"Banking Thorntons?" Bobby asked.

Gib's lips twitched again. "That's right. That's what some people call them. The banking Thorntons. Own the only bank in Longford, matter of fact."

"But how come you're back, Gib?" Bobby's coyote whine had gone higher and wobblier, and his jittery eyes kept flicking from Gib's face to the saddle under the bed. "You didn't skip out, did you?"

Gib's eyes had a teasing squint to them as he answered. "You want to know if I just up and rustled myself a horse and saddle and ran off?" He looked around slowly, at Jacob and Bobby first, and then at each of the other boys, before he shook his head. "Naw," he said, "I didn't run off." His smile spilled over onto his mouth as he added, "And I didn't get here on horseback, either. Matter of fact, I came here in a motorcar."

They stared back, their eyes showing how amazed they were, and how relieved to hear that Gib hadn't done something so dangerous and foolhardy as to run away. At least Bobby and Jacob looked relieved. A couple of the other boys might have been—well, almost disappointed. The way they'd look, perhaps, if a public hanging they were planning to attend had just been called off.

Noticing how one of the new boys had started to ease off toward the dormer windows that faced Lovell Avenue, Gib's smile got wider. "What're you looking to see out there?" he asked. "A sheriff's posse, maybe?"

The new kid looked guilty, but you couldn't really blame him all that much. Wasn't any wonder he was expecting the sheriff or maybe something even worse.

Not after all the things Miss Offenbacher always said about what would happen to runaways.

"Well, what did happen?" Bobby was still whining. "How come you came back?" And then, as his eyes rounded again with a new and even more terrifying thought, "Offenbacher knows you're here, doesn't she?" he whispered, glancing over his shoulder. "You didn't just sneak in, did you, Gib?"

Gib was just opening his mouth to answer when suddenly the whole room was full of a harsh clanging noise. All five of Gib's observers jumped like scared jackrabbits, and then shrugged in embarrassment. Just that noisy old dinner bell, their sheepish smiles said, and with no further hesitation they all trooped out. Everyone but Jacob, who dashed back to give his face a last-minute splash before he rushed after the others, wiping his dripping chin on his shirtsleeves. Gib chuckled, remembering how Jacob always had to be extra careful because dirt showed up so much on his bleached-out skin.

Near the door Jacob paused long enough to ask warily, "You coming, Gib? You coming to supper?"

Gib shook his head. "Nope," he said. "Not tonight. Miss Offenbacher said she wants to talk to everybody first. Kind of explain things, I guess, before the old bad penny shows up again."

"But . . ." Jacob's pale face under its thatch of straw-colored hair was puckered with worry.

Gib went on, "It's all right. I'm not hungry. And anyways, I got something to eat there in my bag."

Jacob went out reluctantly, still looking over his shoulder. It wasn't until they'd all disappeared and their echoing footsteps on the old wooden stairs had faded away to nothing that Gib went back to bed number five. Number five had been Charlie Biggs, if he remembered right. Gib remembered Charlie. A funny-looking kid, with one off-track eye and spiky, no-color hair. Must be ten or eleven years old by now. Gib sighed, wondered about Charlie for a moment, and wished him luck before he sat down on the edge of the bed, pulled out his duffel bag, and took out Mrs. Perry's package.

The sandwiches were full of things no boy at Lovell House ever laid eyes on, lettuce and tomatoes and thick slabs of ham and cheese. They looked mighty good all right, but something was interfering with Gib's appetite. He ate a few bites, then rewrapped the package carefully and put it away. After he'd pulled off his boots, he flopped down on the bed with his arms behind his head, and began to try to face up to the fact that it was really true. He had come to live at the Lovell House orphanage, just as he had done once before—almost six years ago.